The Tunsey Men: Lisette

By
Wendy Stone

Published by
Melange Books, LLC
White Bear Lake, MN 55110
www.melange-books.com

ISBN 978-1-61235-150-6

Credits

Editor: Nancy Schumacher
Copy Editor: Taylor Evans
Format Editor: Mae Powers
Cover Artist: A. Bratt

The Tunsey Men:
Lisette
By
Wendy Stone

Princess Lisette, knowing her evil stepmother wants to kill her, flees the castle and runs into the woods. After a terrifying and exhausting night out, she finds a cottage in the woods owned by the Tunsey brothers. They listen to her tale and agree to allow her to stay. They are all appealing but she falls for the oldest, a man named Gifford. When Gifford finds her in trouble, there is nothing he wouldn't do to save his charming Lisette.

http://threadsofsilk.blogspot.com/
http://www.myspace.com/wendystonesbooks

Also from Wendy Stone at www.melange-books.com.

The Tunsey Men 2, Victoria
The Tunsey Men 3, Giselle

The Tunsey Men:
Lisette
By Wendy Stone

Chapter One

"Find her!"

Lisette heard the sound of her stepmother's voice echoing harshly in the wide common room of the castle. She crouched lower in her hiding place near the stairs, trying to make her slender form disappear. If she were found... It didn't bear thinking of the punishment she would be given this time.

"I cannot believe that you let one lone girl escape your sight," the queen grouched. "I give you so much and ask so little from you." Lisette heard her sigh dramatically. "One small girl and you can not keep her in check. She could ruin everything! I need her found and then I want her killed."

"Yes, your Majesty," the queen's personal guard answered quickly, used to the ways of this royal lady. "It shall be as you wish."

"Ah, but you mustn't do it here. Her father must not hear of this. You must take her out deep into the woods. There you will kill her, bury her body but bring me her hair. I wish to use it to braid into bindings to enchant the king. He will think he killed his daughter and the grief will drive him mad." She laughed the evil sound sending chills of horror down Lisette's spine.

She had to flee and quickly. She couldn't think of letting her father blame himself for her death. He was a good man, though somewhat weak willed which had led him to becoming enchanted by Edwina Hollister's spell to begin with. He'd brought her home, thinking her the perfect woman to become mother to his teenage daughter.

Instead, she'd made Lisette her slave, forcing her to serve morning, noon and night until her back ached and her hands were red and chapped. She was slapped and kicked, pinched

4

cruelly, the bruises hidden by Edwina's witchly craft. Her father saw her as she once was, not the abused and too thin girl she had become.

Dressed in rags, a thin shawl her only protection from the elements and heavy wooden clogs upon her feet, she snuck from the castle, finding her way through what had been her mother's beautiful rose garden, now left to grow wild and choked with weeds. Her heart was in her throat as she found the small iron door in the thick wall that protected the castle, yanking with all her meager strength against the lock until it finally slid back.

She lifted the rusted ring, praying that the door had not grown stuck with corrosion. Pulling, she winced at the loud squeal it made, opening just enough so that she might squeeze her thin body through, pulling it back shut behind her.

She was free! But she could not afford to celebrate her freedom yet, for she was too close to the castle. With a small cry, barely discernable in the noise made by the evening insects, she hurried off, staying close to the wall until she came to where it was closest to the forest. Then she slipped into the woods, unafraid, as thoughts of what she'd left behind her sent her terror spiking more than anything she could face here.

She ran until it grew too dark for her to see one tree from the next and a slight rain began to fall, clouds obscuring the moon. Drawing her ragged shawl closer around her, she sought shelter from the rain under the wide spread branches of a huge tree. There she leaned against its rough bark; her legs curled under her and let her eyes close, too tired to worry about any of the noises coming from the woods around her.

Lisette woke with the first hint of dawn, its pink rays touching on her skin, warming her. Stretching helped to take out the kinks from her unusual sleeping position. Her call of nature was achieved by squatting next to a small bush, her eyes darting furtively around her.

The woods were unfamiliar and she had no idea or which way she'd entered, being turned around in the darkness of the night before. All she could do was pick a direction and hope that it took her further from her stepmother and her cruel ways. Her belly grumbled with hunger and she gave a happy cry when a small berry bush, heaping with the black succulent treat grew close to her path. She ate her fill then took the kerchief off her head, filling it with more of the beautiful berries to eat later. Her fingers grew stained from their juices as did her lips, but she didn't notice. It was the first time in weeks that she could remember her belly not hurting from hunger.

By the time the sun was at its highest peak, Lisette was once more tired, the abuse she'd suffered draining much of her natural stamina and strength from her. When she came upon a tiny clearing in the woods where a cottage stood, its door standing invitingly open, she couldn't resist a peak inside.

"Hello?" she called her voice timid and frightened. Who knew how far the power of her stepmother went?

She received no answer and glanced around. Seeing no one, she stepped inside.

The room was a shambles, dirty clothing and dishes everywhere, boots left to drop dried mud on the wooden floors. Food left sitting out was rotting, cheese turning green with mold. Lisette wrinkled her nose at the smell. Why would anyone want to live in this squalor?

Around a small table were three chairs, all left pushed back from the table. A huge pot of congealing oatmeal sat in the center, bowls left with spoon sitting in them. Lisette picked up one bowl, sniffing at its contents before pulling it away from her face. With a sigh, she dumped the bowls in the pot and took the mess over to the big sink on one wall. A hand pump fed icy water into the sink and she emptied out the pot, filling it with water and hanging it over the still burning fire in the fireplace.

Whoever lived here were terrible housekeepers and worse cooks, she decided. If she were to clean and cook for them, perhaps they would let her stay for a while, at least until she had some idea of what she was going to do next.

She spent the next few hours scrubbing and cleaning, washing clothes, mending holes with the small sewing kit she found tucked away on a shelf. A door in the back of the cottage led to a small basement where food hung in the cooler air. She brought up a slab of meat and some vegetables and sat about making a savory stew, mixing up dough for biscuits to go with it.

By the time she was through, the room shone and smelled fresh and clean, clothes fluttered in the breeze on the line outside and the smell of the stew was drifting through the open doorway. Fluffing the last pillow on the three huge beds she'd found up a ladder into a loft, she yawned hugely, laid down for just a moment on the soft bed and instantly fell asleep.

* * * *

"What's this?" Gifford Tunsey, the oldest of the three Tunsey brothers said as he stared at the smoke coming from the chimney of their cottage. "The fire should have gone out hours ago."

The three brothers were huge men, with long hair and beards that hid most of their faces. Their bodies were hard from the work they did, their manners coarse, for they had been alone since their mother had died ten years before, leaving Giff in charge of raising his brothers.

"Someone done did our laundry," Safford Tunsey said, his eyes going to his underthings now on display on the line. "They left my drawers out where everyone could see."

"What's that smell?" Mallory Tunsey, the youngest, asked, his nose sniffing appreciatively. "It smells kind of like the stew momma used to make."

"That is stew!" Gifford grouched. "Someone's in our house, brothers."

"What we gonna do about it?" Safford asked, his brows knitting as he thought.

"Eat the stew?" Mallory suggested. "It smells really good, Giff."

Gifford just glared and pulled Mallory into the house, his eyes going wide as he saw the spotless and gleaming floor, the neat pile of tidily mended clothing, the dishes that were done and put on the shelf in their rightful places. "Who's done all this?"

"I don't rightly know," Safford mused. "It surely looks good though, kinda like when momma was still alive."

Mallory headed up the ladder, his head peeping over the top to where he could see their beds. "Giff," he hissed in a whisper loud enough to wake the dead. "Someone's in my bed."

"In your bed?" the two brothers down below chorused.

"Well, on my bed. She's a purty little thing. Can I keep her?" Mallory pulled himself up the next couple of steps, hearing his brothers racing up the ladder behind him. She was beautiful, with

7

her red/gold hair blazing in the beam of sunlight that fell across her face, her skin flawless, creamy, the shadows under her eyes standing out in stark relief.

The rags she wore did little to disguise her slender form or the slight swells of her breasts. Her hips were womanly, curving under the skirt she wore, tapering down into the slimmest of ankles and tiny feet shod in harsh wooden shoes. Even as the three brothers stared at her, her eyes fluttered open, as green as the emeralds they hunted for in their hidden cave of treasures.

"Oh," she exclaimed, sitting up and putting her hand to her mouth. "I fell asleep."

"Who are you?" Giff asked, his voice rougher than normal, for the sight of her beauty had brought an ache to his loins.

Lisette cowered back against the headboard, suddenly afraid of the three huge men who hovered over her. "M...my name is L...Lisette," she managed to whisper.

"Did you make the stew?" Mallory asked, his mind still on his stomach.

"Oh, the food, I hope it isn't burned." She clasped her hands to her breasts, not realizing how that emphasized their rounded shape and drew the men's eyes. "I had hoped to impress you with my cleaning and cooking that you might let me stay for a while," she finished, looking up with hope in her innocent eyes.

"Mallory, you go down and check that stew, make sure it ain't burned none. Saf, you go with him." He looked up as Safford seemed ready to argue. "Mind me now," he growled. "I am the oldest."

When they had gone, he reached out his hand, taking the slender fingers of the girl and helping her from the bed. "You aren't from around here. Me and my brothers know of all the females in the area. You definitely ain't one of them. Who are you?"

"My name is L...Lisette. I...I walked a long distance last night," she said quietly, shivering under the stern look in his eyes. "My stepmother wishes me dead," she said at last, the words coming out in a quick rush. "I have no relatives and no where to find shelter. Will you not let me stay?" She glanced up into his harsh, but handsome face, seeing brown eyes that didn't seem moved by her plight at all.

When he stayed silent, she began to move around him. "I will leave now. E…Enjoy the stew," she said with a small sob breaking her words.

"Here now," Giff grouched. "There's no reason to take on now. Let's eat the stew and if it's any good, then we will talk." He noticed that she shivered in the cooler evening air and quickly shed his coat, hanging the huge garment around her shoulders. "It's dirty and it ain't much to look at but it's warm," he said, the gruffness of his voice hiding his emotions.

"Thank you," Lisette said, her eyes shining as the warmth left from his body instantly made her feel better. It was the first kindness she'd received since her father brought her stepmother home and she found herself wanting to cry. A tear slid down her cheek, another quickly following.

"Here now," Giff said. "None of that, it's just a damn jacket."

"I'm sorry," she sniffed, wiping her eyes and gracing him with a smile that had his eyes popping from their sockets. "It's just, well, you are so kind."

"Kind? Giff? Girl you must be in worst shape than we thought," Saff laughed, climbing halfway up to the loft. "The stew's not burned none and there's biscuits to go with it, Giff. Hurry up, we're hungry."

Giff turned, grabbing the arms of an old rocking chair and handing it down to Saff. It was a small rocker, too small for the men to sit in, but it would be perfect for Lisette. "It was our momma's," he said slowly, going down the ladder first and then reaching up for her. He lifted her as if she weighed nothing, feeling her delicate hands settle lightly against his shoulders. He held her for a moment longer than necessary, enjoying the slimness of her waist and the way his hands met around it.

"Put her down, Giff and let's eat."

He did but not before noting the flush on her cheeks. A flush that hadn't been there when they'd been in the loft. Did she maybe like the way he felt, too?

They set up the rocker on the free side of the table, the side across from Giff. Bringing down their bowls, she ladled out the stew, adding biscuits to the top and going to the small basement to bring in a pitcher of icy water. She set it down in front of them and went back to get her own.

When she turned, shock stopped her dead. They were eating like barbarians, scooping the food in and picking up anything that fell on the table to shove in their mouths. As she watched, Saff shoveled an entire biscuit in his mouth, belching loudly and letting the crumbs settle in his matted beard. It was horrifying, disgusting, their manners completely lacking.

Going to the table, she set down her bowl and slammed her hands down on the table.

All three men looked up, surprise in their eyes. "What's wrong with you?" Giff asked.

"What's wrong with me? Look at yourselves. You've got more stew in your beard than in your mouth. Your manners are atrocious and did a single one of you say Grace before you began shoving the food in?" She turned toward Mallory who chuckled as she was yelling at Giff. "And you, did you even wash your hands before you sat down to eat? I just swept this floor and there's dirt all over it again from your boots. Is this the way you three were raised?"

"No, ma'am," he mumbled, his head tipping so that she couldn't see his reddened cheeks. "I'm sorry."

"Go take off your boots and wash your hands, then come back to the table and we'll see if you can eat like a gentleman." She sat down in the rocking chair, her arms crossed over her chest. "That means all of you."

"Now wait a minute, little miss. We don't take kindly to no bossing around in our own house." Giff sat forward, his eyes boring into the pretty green ones of their guest's.

"It's not being bossy if it's only common courtesy," Lisette said smartly, for some reason, completely unafraid of his reaction to her words. "I worked hard today cleaning and cooking. It is only respectful to remove your boots and wash your hands."

Mallory sat back down, quickly followed by Safford. Both had washed under the running water at the hand pump, splashing drops of water everywhere. But their hands were clean and their boots were left by the door where any mud that dropped off could easily be swept outside. They both finished eating quickly, going so far as to take their bowls and spoons to the sink.

Lisette gave Giff a look of askance. "A little washing didn't hurt your brothers," she said smartly, lifting her spoon and taking a careful bite of the stew.

"Ahh, women!" he growled, letting his spoon fall into his bowl and getting up to clump over to the door, kicking his boots off and then running the pump and washing off the dirt of the day. He dried his still grubby hands on a towel, leaving muddy handprints before going back to the table. "Better?" he asked sarcastically.

"It's a start," Lisette said, smiling softly at him in thanks. She took a delicate bite of a biscuit, watching as he sloshed his through his stew then stuffed it in his mouth.

When he caught her watching, he sat straighter in his chair, slowing the flow of food to his mouth with another irritated growl.

Lisette barely hid her smile behind the small square of material she'd found to use as a napkin, finishing up her supper with no more talk. After the meal, she tidied the kitchen, washing the dishes with an economy of motion that she'd learned in her stepmother's kitchens. Wiping away the crumbs, she took them to the doorway and shook them off her raggedy apron, smiling as a pair of birds flittered down to pluck them up quickly, ignoring her presence.

They flew off as a shadow fell over her and she turned to see Giff standing close behind her, close enough that she took a step backwards, losing her balance on the small step off the landing. Her arms pin wheeled once and she would have fallen but he reached out, grabbing her around the waist and hauling her into his arms.

"Oh!" she gasped softly, amazed at the hardness of his body against hers. There seemed no give, as if he were all muscle underneath his soiled shirt and pants.

"Are you all right?" he asked, concern making his voice not quite as harsh. His hand came up, brushing a strand of her red hair from her face as he stared down into her green eyes.

For a moment, it was as if time had ceased to exist, silence fell and even the insects seemed to be holding their breaths. Lisette felt a strange heat suffuse her body, a tingle of attraction that made her nipples harden, and press against the raggedy cloth of her dress.

"W...What?" she breathed, the sound of her voice seeming to break the spell that surrounded them. "Oh, yes," she said softly, pushing back from his arms. "I'm fine."

"Good," he said, steadying her as she stood on her own.

The silence between them seemed to lengthen, growing tense as they stared at each other.

"Did...did you want to say something to me?"

"What? Oh, yeah. Me and my brothers been talking and if you're willing, we'd like you to stay." He ducked his head as her smile dawned on her beautiful face, growing wider until all he wanted to do was haul her back in his arms. She'd felt so wonderful, soft and feminine and she'd smelt like the wild flowers in the field near their cave.

"I'd really like that," she said, her eyes sparkling.

"Good, then it's settled. We decided that tomorrow we'll build you a bed of your own. But for tonight, you can sleep with me in mine." Giff turned as he finished speaking, never noticing the look of fear that came to her eyes.

"I...I can't sleep with you," she said slowly, her body shaking as fear, harsh and palpable, flooded her. "It isn't proper."

"It's just for tonight," Giff said, turning back with a quizzical look upon his face. "You don't...think...You do. No, it's just sleeping. I'd sleep with one of my brothers but two of us in one bed just don't work well. Since I'm the oldest, you'll sleep with me."

Lisette worried her lower lip with her teeth, a habit she'd had for many years when she was uncertain or afraid. "Just sleeping?" she asked slowly.

"Just sleeping," he confirmed. "You didn't bring anything with you besides what's on your back, did you?"

"No. I...I had to leave in a hurry."

"Well then, for tonight you can borrow one of my shirts to sleep in. Tomorrow, I'll dig up momma's old trunk and you can see what you can do with her old clothes. Should be some material in that trunk too," he said thoughtfully.

The thought of clean clothes, even if they were second hand, was almost more than she could take. She clasped her hands against her breasts, overwhelmed by the generosity of these huge men. "I don't know how to thank you."

"Just keep cooking like you did tonight. That's thanks enough." He grasped her arm loosely, steering her back into the cottage. "In the trunk in front of my bed are my extra shirts. Why don't you go up and get ready for bed. When you're ready, just call down and we'll come up."

She nodded, hurrying to the ladder and scurrying up quickly. The trunk in front of his bed was huge, like everything that had to do with the brothers. She strained to lift the top, finding a passel of shirts just tossed inside. Nothing was folded and she could see that there would be much more mending for her to do just in this one trunk. Lifting out one of his shirts, she held it up to her diminutive frame, marveling that what fit him so well would hang like one of her dresses on her.

Shedding the worn and stained dress and the single petticoat she wore under it, she slid the shirt on over her head, buttoning up the placard with fingers that trembled. The hem reached her knees and she had to roll up the sleeves many times to uncover her hands. Still, it was less than a proper outfit for her to be wearing in the company of men.

She hurried and slid under the heavy comforter of Giff's bed, calling in a hesitant voice. "I'm in bed."

Candles were extinguished and the men's voices grew closer as they climbed the ladder. Mall stopped at the edge of Giff's bed, his eyes drawn to the tiny beauty huddled under the sheets. "You are very pretty, Miss Lisette."

"Thank you, Mr. Mallory," she said primly, holding the covers up to her chin.

Giff came up behind him and slapped him on the back of his head. "Go to bed," he growled, feeling anger flood him at his brother's words.

"Je—s-us, Giff, what'd you go and do that for?" Mall rubbed the back of his head. "I was just being friendly."

"You be friendly tomorrow when she's fully dressed, until then, get to bed!" he roared.

Safford chuckled as he walked past his brother. "I think Giff got bit by the love bug," he said when he was too far away for his brother to reach him.

"I'm going to show you who got bit," Giff growled. "Now the two of you get to bed. Dawn ain't going to wait." He blew out the

13

candle he'd brought up with him, leaving them in the dark except for the faint glow of the fire down below.

Lisette heard the rustle of clothing and then the men sighing in their beds, rolling and moving pillows. She could still see the faint outline of Giff as he stood at the end of the bed, his eyes on her face.

"You might want to close your eyes, girl. I ain't going to sleep in these clothes."

"Oh," she gasped, her eyes slamming shut so quickly that it brought a chuckle to the gruff man. She huddled under the covers, hearing him taking off his clothes. Unable to resist, she peaked through her eyelashes, barely stifling another gasp as his shirt slid off his massive shoulders.

His chest was hard, sculptured like the statues that were in her mother's garden of the Greek Gods. His stomach rippled with strength, his arms bulged as he moved with conservative movements. She watched as his hands went to the waistband of his pants and he slowly unbuttoned the fastening, letting them drop to the floor. Even as he stepped out of them, he was tugging on the soft cotton drawers he wore under them, pulling them off as well.

When he turned, Lisette caught her breath. She was no longer the innocent Princess she'd been before Edwina had moved into the castle, having been exposed to the rougher and crasser class of people that would couple or answer the call of nature within her eyesight. But she'd never seen any man who looked like this.

His thighs were strong and wide, heavily muscled and as big around as her waist. His legs were long and well defined. But what amazed her the most was the sight of his cock, lying against his thigh, it was easily the biggest she'd ever seen.

She felt her face go hot, her breath seemed to strangle in her lungs and her eyes opened wide.

"I thought you weren't going to look?" he whispered, feeling a stirring in his loins as his eyes met hers.

"I...I'm sorry," she said quickly, rolling over to lie on her side with her back to him, her red face buried in one of the pillows. She thought she heard him chuckle, but it could have been the heavy beat of her heart pounding inside her head. She closed

14

her eyes, opening them quickly when she felt the mattress move, sinking lower, and causing her body to roll towards him.

"Oh," she cried, moving back to her side of the bed. "Maybe this wasn't such a good idea."

"It'll be fine," Giff growled, punching his pillow into submission. "Go to sleep. We get up before the chickens here."

She tried, she really did. Perhaps it was the long nap in the afternoon or maybe the strangeness of being in bed with a man, but she couldn't sleep. At first, she laid as still as she could, afraid to take a deep breath in case she disturbed him. Soon the sound of his snores mixed with the grunts and snores of his brothers to create a cacophony of sound.

It should have irritated her. Instead, she found the sound of the three men almost soothing. Lisette couldn't remember the last time she'd felt safe. Being in the same room with Gifford, Safford and Mallory made her feel that way now. She closed her eyes, listening to the sound, and smiled.

That smile turned to a whispery shriek when Giff rolled in the bed, his hand coming out and landing on her stomach. Then it was as if he homed in on her, moving towards the warmth of her body until he was wrapped around her, pulling her into his arms.

"Giff," she whispered, poking his hard chest carefully with one finger. She poked him harder when all he did was snort and then buried his face in her hair. "Giff," she hissed, trying not to wake up Safford and Mallory. "Wake up."

"Hmm?" he muttered sleepily. He grunted, rolling back to his side of the bed. "Sorry."

She took a deep breath, strangely missing the way he'd felt against her. Rolling to her side, she kept her back to him and forced her eyes closed. Before long, she slept.

* * * *

Giff woke to the feel of soft warmth against his body, the scent of wildflowers intoxicating his senses and a small hand resting against his chest, the palm rubbing gently against his flat nipple. He stared down, his eyes adjusted to the dark. Lisette.

Sometime during the night, she'd scooted toward him, perhaps attracted to his warmth, but now, for whatever reason, she lay in his arms, her head cradled against the crook of his neck. He could feel her lower half, bared by the twisted shirt that rode up around her waist, pressing against his hip, her thigh lying over his own.

His body responded with a vengeance, his cock hardening in a rush of heated blood, tenting the covers over him. He could feel the slight swell of her breasts pressed against his side and he wanted to turn, to nuzzle that soft flesh with his mouth, take a pert nipple between his lips, taste of her sweetness. A groan tore from him, and his arms tightened as he fought to control the lustful urgings that were swamping him.

His hand seemed to move with a will of its own, sliding from her slender waist down to the soft flesh of her bottom cheeks. Her skin was as soft as silk against his calloused palm and he forced himself to still, afraid that she'd wake and scream at finding herself in this position with him.

Giff glanced down, seeing her exquisite face so close, framed by those beautiful red/gold curls. Her lips were lush, parted with her sleeping breaths, her teeth white and even. Her lashes rested softly against her rosy cheeks, fluttering as she dreamed.

Slowly, trying desperately not to wake her, he pulled away, carefully cradling her head until he could pull a pillow down and put it under her. Then he moved further away, turning until he could watch her face while she slept.

She had a look of refinement about her, the look of a lady. He couldn't help but sigh, that look meant she was much too good for a peasant such as he. Nothing could happen between the two of them. She would stay here until some wandering Prince saw her, sweeping her up on his white destrier and taking her away with him to his castle to live there happily ever after. Even the thought was depressing. With a muttered growl, he turned away from her, struggling against the desire that still raged in his body, finally falling back to sleep.

* * * *

It was early; even the morning birds had not yet risen, when Lisette woke with a start, feeling more refreshed than she'd felt in months. Her body didn't ache from constant abuse, she had no new bruises or whip marks and she'd found a new home. She sighed, stretching luxuriously.

16

Her hips bumped against something in the bed, and she paused, puzzled. Her confusion lasted mere seconds for Giff turned toward her in his sleep, pulling her back so that her body was curled into his, her rounded buttocks cradled against his hips. His hand slipped under the loose fabric of her shirt and he mumbled as his palm slid over the soft curve of her breast, her nipple hardening against his calloused skin.

She whimpered at the sensations that tore through her, strange and terrifyingly intense, echoing in the pit of her stomach and creating a strange ache in her loins. She wriggled against him even as his fingers sought and found the puckered bud, rolling it gently.

"Mm, Lisette," he murmured, sighing in his sleep as his fingers took liberties that he'd declared forbidden for himself earlier. He played with her delicate nipple then slid his palm down the flat line of her stomach, curving it over her hip and then pressing between her thighs.

"Gifford," she gasped, whimpering as he sifted through the bright red curls at the apex of her thighs, pushing his fingers against the damp flesh of her slit. It should have shocked her, the familiarities he was taking with her most intimate flesh, but instead, she moved against him, unable to stop herself when the pleasure was so great. Lifting her upper leg, she let it rest against his, opening herself to him in invitation for more.

Giff's finger was deliciously hard and maddeningly soft at the same time. She felt him slip it through her wetness, gathering it on the tip before using it to circle some small part of her that had her hips jerking and lightning shooting through her. She couldn't help but rock against him, her breathing coming in short heated pants.

He woke with a start, his fingers buried in the heated dampness that was between her thighs. Her hands were holding onto his wrist as if unsure whether to pull away or hold him to her. She was writhing against him, her bottom rubbing over his hard cock. He wanted so badly to pull her back further, to push into the heat and tightness of her pussy from behind and ride her until they were both too satiated to move.

With a groan of pure need, he slid his finger down further, finding her small opening and pushing gently inside. "You are

17

still a virgin," he growled, finding the tiny membrane that kept him from her.

"Y...yes, she moaned, turning her face to look at him despite the blush that stole over her cheeks.

His curse was low and heartfelt. He drew away from her, though it was the hardest thing he'd ever done, leaving that tight, wet cunny intact. He would have been her first. That thought made his cock jerk and his heart quicken even more.

He rose from the bed, grabbing his drawers and breeches from the floor and pulling them on even though it was still a good hour before he usually arose. "Go back to sleep," he growled, ignoring the chill in the room and heading down the ladder.

Lisette buried her face in the pillow, groaning at the lingering scent of his body. It was a manly smell of earth and work and a spicy aroma that she couldn't name. It made her body tremble more until she knew she couldn't lie abed. Rising, she slid into her old clothing, quickly and quietly making the bed and laying his old shirt across the foot.

Then she hurried down the ladder as well.

He stood in the open doorway, staring up at the sky as it lightened and the stars lost their incredible light in the face of the dawning sun. Giff had hoped that the cold air of morning would cool his ardor, but as he heard her light tread behind him, he knew he was fooling himself. The only thing that would cool his desire for her would be to bury his cock in that tight little cunny and loose himself in her.

But he couldn't. Lisette hadn't spoken of her past, but he could see that she was more than he, blue blooded no matter the rags upon her back or the plight that had put them there. She was a lady, and he was a big, rough, uncouth miner.

Lisette went to the fire, stirring up the embers he'd banked the night before and stacking small pieces of wood upon them to get the fire started once more. When she reached for the bigger pieces, she found him there before her.

"Let me," he growled. "You start the water for coffee."

She nodded, here eyes searching his face before she turned to do his bidding, unsure of what she'd seen there. He didn't seem angry. But there had been a look in his eyes, maybe of sadness? She couldn't be sure.

She pumped water into the huge old kettle, bringing it to the fire to swing it over on one of the two hooks embedded in the stone of the hearth. Then she brought out the huge pot and made ready to fix the oatmeal that seemed to be the staple for breakfast.

"If you had some chickens, I could fix eggs in the morning," she said suddenly, breaking the quiet between them.

"Who'd care for the silly birds?" he growled. "We don't have the time."

"I...I could, if you still want me to stay."

She glanced his way as she measured out oatmeal and then added in a handful of raisins she had found in the cellar.

"Listen, Lisette..." Giff began, only to shut his mouth as he heard his brothers rustling around in the loft. "Yes, we still want you to stay," he said instead. "I'll see about getting you some chickens."

He went back to the ladder, climbed up to grab his shirt and socks, yelling at Saff and Mall as they were fighting to hurry up. Lisette ducked outside, going to the small privy at the back of the cottage. When she came back in, all three men had slicked back their hair at the pump, washed and were sitting at the table, waiting for breakfast.

She stirred the oatmeal, brought the huge pot of coffee to the table, and then dished out huge servings for the men. They ate quickly, speaking little. When they were finished, Mall stacked the dishes and took them to the sink, before thanking Lisette for breakfast. Hurrying into his boots, he picked up the pickaxe he'd left by the door the night before and waited for his brothers.

Saff finished his coffee, then leaned down and pressed a kiss to Lisette's pretty cheek. "Thank you, it was much better than Giff's oatmeal. We can usually use what we don't eat to caulk the holes in the walls."

She giggled as he'd meant her to and then he too was out the door.

"Stay close to the house, Lisette. We'll be home early this afternoon to make you a bed. And I'll see to your chickens. Momma's trunk is in the cellar along the back wall, if you want to look through it. That should keep you occupied." He went to walk by her, only to stop suddenly, grabbing her arms and pulling her close to him. His lips found hers, brushing over them quickly and then he let her go, stomping into his boots and closing the door behind him.

Lisette dropped into her chair, her face flushing. She could still feel the gentleness of his kiss and she waved her hand in front of her face trying to cool it off. "Oh my," she whispered. Then with a spring in her step, she rose from the chair and started her chores.

Chapter Two

It was a different looking Lisette they came home to that evening. She'd found a pretty dress that only took a bit of altering to fit her slender form. Going through the trunk had given her a new brush and mirror as well as a box of hairpins. She'd taken the time to clean up, brushing her long unruly hair and pinning it into a mass of curls at the top of her head.

Then she got to work, wrapping an apron she'd also found in the trunk around her slender waist and filling the washtub full of hot water. She washed clothing first washing even the rags she'd been wearing, figuring that they could be used for dusting if they were clean. Bringing in the clothing she'd washed yesterday, she hung the freshly laundered wash out in the stiff breeze and warm sun, humming as she worked.

The day was warm and the air around the cottage was fresh with the scent of the woods and the smell of flowers. She skipped around to the back of the cottage, picking a handful of the pretty yellow daisies to put in the small vase she'd found for the table.

For a while, she basked in the rays of the sun, enjoying the freedom of doing as she pleased after having to do her stepmother's bidding for so very long. Then she went back into the cottage, pleased to be cooking and cleaning because it was what she wanted to do.

The floors gleamed; the table had been scrubbed of years of accumulated dirt and a roast of venison cooked in the small oven set into the wall of the hearth. She'd begun to go to the door, watching for her men to arrive home for the day. Gifford had said they would be home early as they were planning on building her a bed of her own today.

That thought sent a bevy of butterflies to flit in her stomach, reminding her of the night before and the way he'd felt against her, his finger pressing inside of her body making her feel so very strange. Her cheeks heated and a flush stole its way across her face. If he hadn't stopped, would she have been strong enough to stop him?

Before she could decide upon an answer, she heard deep male voices. For a moment, she thought of hiding, but then she recognized Gifford at the lead of the three men, his shovel held over his shoulder, dirt smudged across his cheeks and loose in his hair. Excitement made her heart race and she wondered not for the first time that day if he'd thought of her at all.

"Lisette?" he called as they entered the clearing.

She went to the door, opening it and standing shyly in the doorway. "You're home," she said unnecessarily, blushing when she realized how it had sounded.

"You had no problems today?" he asked, walking up to her, unable to drag his eyes from her.

"No, none." Her eyes met his and she felt a strange flutter inside.

"Are you two gonna stand there making goo goo eyes at each other all night or can some of us that are hungry come in to eat," Safford said, knocking Giff in the back with his shoulder.

"Oh," she said, hurrying to back from the door. "Take off your boots by the door and wash up. Dinner will be ready in a just a few minutes."

She was so flustered that she went to the oven, reaching for the handle without picking up the heavy mitten, burning her fingers. Her cry of pain was barely uttered before Giff was there, lifting her hand to look at the burn.

"Cold water," he ordered her, taking her to the pump. "Hold your hand there, Lisette."

He pumped water over her red fingers, turning to yell at his brothers. "Saff, take that roast outta the oven. Mall, go get some of that salve that momma made and bring me some bandages." They rushed to do his as he ordered.

"Does it hurt?" he asked her softly.

"No, my pride hurts worse. I know better than to touch the door like that. I...I wasn't thinking," she whispered, glancing up at him.

"It was an accident," he said. "It wasn't your fault."

He dried her hand tenderly, gentle around the reddened burn. Then he took the salve from Mallory. "It don't smell too nice but it helps the pain and will make it heal much quicker. My momma was famous for her healing poultices, salves and unguents." He scooped up a dab of the greasy white paste, smearing it gently on the burn before wrapping her hand with the bandages. "Gotta keep it clean and dry so we'll be doing the dishes and such for the next few days until you heal up some."

"Oh no, really, I can do them. I have to earn my keep," she said, a note of panic in her voice.

"Lisette, we aren't going to kick you out just cause you can't do dishes. Calm down," Gifford smiled, his teeth white against the dark of his beard.

"But..." she stopped when she saw the look in his brown eyes. "Very well. I'll wait until my hand feels better."

He finished tying the last knot, lifting her hand to check the bandage. Then he lifted it to his mouth, kissing it softly.

Lisette felt her cheeks heat again at the unexpected sweetness of his kiss, feeling flustered as she dropped her eyes, unable to look at him. "Thank you," she whispered.

"You're welcome." He dropped her hand when he heard Mallory laugh, turning her head to see both his brothers watching them. "Let's eat," he growled, glaring at the two.

The brothers were on their best behavior that evening, making Lisette laugh with their jests and playful jibes. Gifford sat next to her, cutting her meat into bite-sized pieces for her, filling her glass and buttering her bread. His eyes constantly turned to her, seeming captivated by the melodic trill of her laughter, the sparkle of her eyes, the pretty smile on her face.

Even when everyone had eaten their fill, no one rose right away to leave the table, instead sitting around talking and laughing until a yawn snuck up on Lisette. She barely had time to cover her mouth.

"You're tired," Gifford said, leaning closer to her. "We didn't get to the bed. Will you be uncomfortable sleeping in my bed one more night?"

Lisette shook her head, a blush causing a rosy flush on her face. "No, I'll be fine."

"Clean up the dishes," he told Safford.

Mallory grinned, only to frown when Giff looked at him. "You can dry."

While the two younger brothers cleaned up the dinner mess, Lisette went to the corner where the big wash tub was stored, yanking it out to the middle of the floor with one hand. "Would you fill the kettle and the big pot with water to warm please?" she asked Safford.

"You wanna bath right now?" Giff asked, his brows furrowing together.

"No, you do before I'd even think of getting into bed with you again." She frowned as she heard her own words, realizing how they sounded.

"But...it's not Saturday," he grouched.

"I don't care what day it is, you are filthy, and when is the last time someone cut your hair or trimmed your beard?" She stood in front of him, her hands resting on her hips.

"It don't need to be cut none," he grumped, but the words were muttered as if he were afraid of making Lisette mad.

Then when was the last time you ran a brush through it?"

"No one cares what we look like. We're in a mine all day long, working. Who cares what my hair looks like?"

"I do," Lisette said softly, shutting him up. "All three of you need baths and hair cuts."

"But your hand..." Giff began to protest.

"...will be fine to hold a pair of scissors. The longer you argue, the longer it'll take," she said reasonably.

Mallory poured the now steaming water into the huge tub while Lisette brought out towels and a bar of scented soap. It smelled of sandalwood and myrrh, a pleasing combination though Lisette wouldn't use it on herself.

"Now, you get undressed while my back is turned and get into the tub. While you wash, I'll cut your hair and then you can wash it." She primly turned her back, hearing him sigh heavily before the rustle of clothing being removed. She waited until she heard the splash of the water and his sigh as he settled into the tub, then she turned.

For a moment, all she could see was the wide expanse of his chest, the rippled muscles of his abdomen and his brown eyes staring at her with a hint of malice. A blush rose to her cheeks and she couldn't help but wonder if she'd be rosy cheeked for the rest of her life as much blushing as she did here.

"S...see, that's not so bad now, is it?" She went to where she'd laid out the scissors and comb, grabbing one of the large towels and using it to cover his shoulders.

"What are you doing?" he yelped, feeling her hands on his head.

"Cutting your hair, settle down, it won't hurt."

She started in the back, chopping off the too long locks. They fell to the floor and more were added as she moved around him, clipping and combing until she was pleased with the effect. Then she grabbed a handful of the long straggly beard, lopping it off before he could protest.

"Hold on!" he cursed the air blue, his hand going up to feel the ends of his now short beard. "Do you know how long those take to grow?"

"Too long, if you ask me. Now hold still," she said, trimming and snipping, a smile growing on her face as she finished the last cut. "Now wash." She handed him the bar of soap and went to get the broom, cleaning up the hair and putting it all in a small cloth bag.

Gifford grouched and groaned, refusing to tell Lisette how light his head felt now that she'd cut off his long hair. He washed quickly, cursing more when Safford brought over a bucket of cool water to rinse the soap off his hair. When he was done, he stood, Lisette, turning quickly, wrapped the wide towel around his waist. He stepped out of the tub and onto the towel she'd left on the floor to catch any drips.

"You look like a shorn rat," Safford chuckled gleefully.

"Safford, would you and Mallory empty the water out back while I set another pot to heat?" Lisette asked sweetly. "You're next."

"What....nuh uh, no, you ain't cutting my hair," he cursed, backing away from her.

"Quit being a baby and empty the water," she ordered.

"Giff, make her stop," Safford whined, his eyes never leaving the slim beauty as she stood patiently, her arms crossed in front of her.

"Do as you're told," Giff growled, enjoying Safford's predicament after his own shearing.

With a lot of cursing and cussing, Safford emptied the tub, filled it and sat, resigned under Lisette's skillful hand. Then it was Mall's turn. Instead of arguing, he got eagerly into the tub, enjoying having Lisette's total attention upon him. By the time she was done, the bag of hair was rounded out and her three men looked completely different.

She'd cut their hair short, tapering it so that it would stay out of their eyes. Silky now that it was clean, it lay against their well-shaped heads, drawing the eye to their handsome faces. The scraggly facial hair was gone; instead, trimmed and shaped beards graced their chins, framing strong mouths. The three of them like this was enough to take any girl's breath and Lisette wasn't immune to their charms.

"Will you empty the tub, please?" she asked Giff, dropping her eyes from his handsome face. "Then you can all go to bed. I'm going to take my bath."

Giff's eyes opened wide as he thought about her, sitting in that tub, naked, her body glistening in the light from the fire. He hurried to stand, taking one end of the tub, and dragging it out the door. Emptying it took seconds and then he brought it back in, dumping the heated water in and pumping more to heat for her to rinse with.

"Bed," he growled at the other two, who still stood where they'd been when he'd left with the tub.

"But...she got to watch us take baths," Mallory complained good-naturedly, ducking the fist that came flying at his face. "All right, we're going," he said with a put upon sigh.

He scurried up the ladder followed quickly by Safford. Giff stared at the ladder, waiting. "I don't hear you getting into bed," he growled.

Seconds later, two mattresses rustled, the ropes under them groaning as they took the weight of the men.

"I'm sorry about those dunderheads." He turned towards Lisette, seeing her eyes quickly drop to the floor from where she'd been staring at his still bare back. A teasing grin came to his lips, a spark of interest gleamed in his eyes. "Need any help with your fastenings?"

Instead of answering, she turned, exposing her slender back and the long row of buttons that did up the back of the dress. It had taken her forever to get them buttoned; she'd never be able to undo them with her hand like it was.

Giff took a step toward her, his hands coming up to touch the first button. He scowled as he saw they were trembling. He felt like an untried schoolboy around the pretty maid. Taking a deep breath, he slipped one tiny disk from its hole and then another, exposing a line of pale flesh that covered her spine.

Lisette held her breath, feeling his fingers brushing against her skin, a shiver of longing sending goose flesh over her body. It seemed to take forever for him to finish the task, though it was probably only seconds. Holding the bodice up in the front with her hand, she turned. "Thank you."

"You're welcome," he said, his deep voice growing even huskier. "If you need anything else, I'll be close. Leave the water and I'll dump it in the morning." He turned toward the ladder, knowing if he stayed with her any longer he'd give into his body's violent urgings to sweep her into his arms and kiss her, tearing away the interfering material of her dress and make her his. Every pore of his body wanted her, wanted to drown in her sweet scent, in the silkiness of her hair, in the heat of her body. He had to get out of there, now!

He was at the ladder when he couldn't help but glance back, watching as she turned her back to him, dropping the gown to the floor and picking it up with her un-bandaged hand. A low groan rumbled deep in his chest and he couldn't move, his eyes greedily devouring the sight of her slim back, the shapely curve of her shoulders, the full heaviness of her breast. A petticoat hid everything from the waist down, but as he watched, her fingers slipped to the ties that held it to her slender waist.

He would be damned to hell for his spying, he knew. But nothing could have made him move from that spot. He saw her hand pull at the laces, saw her loosening the soft fabric and watched it fall to the ground in a heap of off white material. She stepped out of it, bending over to pick it up and he thought he'd go up in flames.

Her backside was round and firm with two tiny dimples that seemed to beg for his kiss. As she bent, he could see red curls and the swollen lips they framed. He swallowed heavily, feeling light headed and realized he'd forgotten to breathe as he watched this perfect vision ready herself for her bath.

When she plucked the pins from her hair, letting the long locks tumble down around her shoulders, he burned to bury his hands there, remembering how soft and silky they had felt against his skin the night before. He wanted to kiss her, to touch her, to find out what color her nipples were and how she tasted.

His thoughts came to a careening halt when she stepped into the tub and he knew she'd be turning around. She would see him there; she wouldn't be able to miss him. He turned again, grabbing the ladder and was at the top in seconds, even as she settled into the heated water with a sigh.

Standing at the top of the loft, he couldn't help but take one last look.

"She's real pretty, ain't she, Giff?" Mallory smirked from his bed.

"Giff would know, he's been down there with her forever."

"Shut up you two and mind your own damn business," Giff grouched, turning and going to his bed, the bed he would share again tonight with their beautiful housekeeper.

"It is our damn business," Saff said, sitting up and staring at him. "If'n you chase her away with your lusting, who's going to cook and clean for us? I don't want to go back to the way it was around here."

"I'm not going to chase her away. Just…just shut up and go to sleep. We got that new vein to explore tomorrow."

"If'n Giff don't want her none, could I have her?" Mall asked.

"No!" both Giff and Saff snapped.

"Je-sus," Mall drawled. "I was just asking."

* * * *

Lisette's father, King Maxim, stared down at the oval of ivory he held in his hands that held the portrait of his deceased wife. His eyes traced the heart shape of her face, lighting on the green of her eyes and the sparkle that the artist had caught with such detail they almost seemed alive. "I miss you, Nathalie," he whispered to the portrait. "I've failed our daughter and dirtied your memory. I'm so sorry."

His voice was filled with remorse and self-scorn, but his hands were careful as he replaced the portrait in its place of honor on the fireplace mantle in his bedroom. Edwina had thrown a huge tantrum the first time she'd discovered it there, but since they no longer shared a bed, he felt no need to remove it.

Edwina, he sighed, thinking of his wife. "She was a huge mistake, Nathalie. I should have known that there was no one that could replace you in my heart or in Lisette's. But I was so lonely without you and I know Lisette needed a woman's hand to tame her wild ways. Now she's disappeared. Is she dead, my love? Is our daughter now with you?"

He paused, seeming to wait for an answer that would never come. "I wish you could guide me now as you did when you were alive." He kissed the tips of his fingers, laying them gently upon the lush painted lips of his wife's portrait. "Watch out for her, love."

He left his chamber, heading down the wide halls toward the main gathering room. It was where he heard the complaints of his people, accepting their gracious gifts and deciding disputes. Today, he would be summoning all the men of his lands to help in the search for his lovely Lisette. He had to know why she had run away.

When he entered the gathering room, a large crowd of men went to their knees in front of him. He bowed his head, distracted, and made his way to his throne, not seeing the man who stood just off to the side of his throne.

"Your Highness," he said as soon as he saw the king. "Might I beg a word with you?"

"Now isn't a good time," the king said, waving his hand at the man. "My daughter has disappeared and we must find her before something untoward happens to her."

"I come to you now because of your daughter."

He backed up a step as the King's head raised. "What do you know of her disappearance?" he asked, rage making his blue eyes icy. "If you've hurt her…"

"No…oh no, your Highness. I have no idea of your daughter's whereabouts. I come to you on a different matter. My Prince, Prince Rodbert the third of the Gorham principality, wishes to petition you for Princess Lisette's hand in marriage."

"I cannot think of such things now," King Maxim growled. "My daughter is missing, man. Did you not hear me say that?"

29

"Yes, but if you will commit to a marriage between the two, my Prince will send men to help search, perhaps come to find her himself. Would that not make the search easier?"

"He will send men?" the king asked. His lands were vast and mostly wooded, far from the villages where the peasants raised their crops. It would take the men of his lands forever to search every mile. More men might find her more quickly.

"Yes, your Highness. It would but take your signature upon this contract and Prince Rodbert will happily lend his men to your cause." He held out the elegantly rolled scroll sealed with a blob of bright red wax, a seal of Gorham's principality etched into it.

Maxim took the scroll, his fingers unsteady as he broke the seal. He held it in front of him, reading over the words that had been written there. Glancing back at the Prince's representative, he cocked one regal eyebrow. "This is more than a fair offer, sir. Has the Prince been introduced to my daughter?"

"No sire, but all know of her beauty and sweet disposition. Joining the two lands by the bonds of marriage will strengthen both kingdoms and allow for trade between our villages."

"What of this Prince Rodbert? Is he fair and kind? Will he be good to my daughter?"

"He is known as the Charmed Prince for he was born with a fair face and an ease of manners that have the ladies swooning. He is manly with sword and steed and settles disputes with insight beyond his years. Prince Rodbert is sought after by many of the royals as husband to their daughters, but he would hear of none but Princess Lisette."

"And he *will* send men?"

"Surely, your Highness. It takes but your signature and I shall send word to the Prince. You shall have your extra men within hours."

Maxim closed his eyes, struggling with what would be right. He'd never thought to marry his daughter off this young, instead wanting to keep her with him for a few more years before giving her up to a husband. But if Prince Rodbert's men could help in finding her, he would be a fool not to accept this offer. "Very well," he said, reaching out to his scribe for the man's quill and ink. He scratched his name to the bottom of the scroll, sanding it carefully before rolling it back up and sealing it next to the original seal with his own crest.

"It is done."

"Thank you, Highness. I shall inform the Prince of your decision." He bowed deeply then backed away, turning when he reached the door.

"What have you done?"

Maxim turned, seeing Edwina standing next to him, her eyes glaring and icy. At one time, he'd thought she was beautiful, congratulating himself at choosing another wife that was beautiful and sweet. Now he knew her beauty covered a heartless breast. She was cruel and hateful, finding any number of ways to make him sorry he'd ever married her.

"I have signed a contract of marriage between Lisette and Prince Rodbert. It will be a good match and Rodbert has promised help in finding Lisette." He turned his head, hoping she would take the hint and go away.

Instead, she moved closer, her long slender fingers clawing at the doublet he wore. "You've made promises you cannot keep, Maxim. For all that we know, Lisette is dead, the victim of a thief's lust or a beast's hunger. She could be broken and bleeding at the bottom of some ravine, never to wake. What will happen then?"

"Perhaps I shall give you to him in her place then," Maxim snarled. "Though that might bring about a war between our kingdoms for you certainly would drive the man as mad as you have me."

Edwina pulled herself up, straightening her spine as she heard his words. "I have been a loving and true wife in all way."

Maxim scoffed, his lips turning up into a sneer of derision. "I should have divorced you when I first saw what you were, Edwina. I didn't because I was worried about my reputation and that of my bloodline. If I find out that you had anything to do with Lisette's disappearance. Let me just say, no one will mourn your loss."

"Maxim!" she cried, her hand going to her breast. "I cannot believe…"

"Stop," he ordered tiredly. "I do not have it in me to listen to any more of your excuses and half truths. Just know that I promise you will pay, and pay endlessly, if any harm befalls my daughter. Now, leave. I must give my men their orders." He waved her away, ignoring the scowl upon her face and the anger in her eyes.

Edwina turned, rage burning in her breast. She stormed away, pushing aside a peasant who did not get out of her way quickly enough. Grabbing Geoffrey, her lover and coconspirator, she dragged him away from the rest, pulling him through the corridors and to her room. As soon as her door closed, she turned on him, her long, sharp nails digging into the fabric of his shirt. "You must find that little brat now!"

"I've been searching for her, my love," Geoffrey said, trying to placate the irate queen. "There has been no sight of her, no footprints, no fabric or anything. It is as if she disappeared."

"Someone had to see her leave the castle. She took nothing but the clothes on her back, no food, no provisions of any kind. There is no way she could survive all this time on her own." Edwina pushed away from Geoffrey, pacing the floor distractedly. "But I feel she is still there, waiting to show up at the worst possible moment. You must look harder, Geoffrey. Find her for me."

"I will do my best, my queen." He bowed before her before taking her in his arms and kissing her soft lips. "Do not worry, it will give you wrinkles," he teased.

"Wrinkles?" she asked, her brow furrowing. "Wrinkles!"

"I but jested, truly. You are the most beautiful woman, the most graceful, and intelligent," he said quickly, trying to placate her because he knew what her anger was like. "I will start now, my queen, and won't return until I find her."

"Fine," Edwina said, waving her hand at him as he tried to pull her close once more.

He left, feeling a sudden relief at being away from her. Perhaps it was time for him to leave this kingdom?

Edwina went to her mirror, gazing into the wavy reflective surface. Her fingers traced the fine lines that were beginning to show at the corner of her eyes, patting the flesh under her sharp chin. A scowl caused a deep line to appear between her eyes and she turned away from the mirror, going to the trunk at the foot of her bed.

Lifting the lid, she pulled a huge leather bound tome from its depths. She shifted it to her other arm, holding it closely to her like a precious possession, setting it carefully upon her dressing table. Holding her hand above the book, she took a deep breath and picked up a sharpened pin. The tip pricked her finger, going deep. Blood welled, forming a bright red drip upon the pale pink of her finger. Holding it over the huge book, she let it fall onto the bound leather cover.

Book of spells, my blood I feed. Show to me the spell I need.

The book opened, the cover rattling down on the wooden surface of the table. Pages flickered, flipping past as if a wild wind held the book in its thrall. Then it settled upon a single page, a ribbon slithering from the spine of the book to mark the place.

The same bloody finger slid over the spell, finding the contents of the potion needed. Even as her blood fell upon the page, it disappeared into the paper. Her gift, just as it was her mother's gift and her mother before that, to feed the book, to gift it with her own blood and to gain the knowledge within.

"Oh ho, what is this?" she chuckled, her laugh sounding decidedly like a cackle. "To be gifted with the spell of youth, a young innocent must be sacrificed. Oh, this is wonderful. I will be beautiful and get rid of that blasted girl at the same time."

Her laughter rang out, filling the room, scaring a young maid who was about to enter the room. She shuddered in distaste, turning quickly away.

Chapter Three

She sank into the steamy water with a sigh. Lisette was tired, but it was the good kind of tired that came from a day of working hard and knowing you'd accomplished something.

Hearing a noise, she turned her head, seeing Giff's back as he reached the top of the ladder. For a moment, she narrowed her eyes in confusion. Hadn't he gone up there before? Had he been down here watching her undress? Surely not, she would have heard him, wouldn't she?

Her heart fluttered at the thought of him seeing her nude, remembering the way his hands had felt upon her body last night. She hadn't been able to deny him anything; his touch had been fire, setting her to craving something that she didn't understand. As she watched, he moved away from the ladder and she heard the murmur of deep voices from above. Then the bed creaked and it became silent. Lying back in the water with only the hiss and pop of the fire for company, Lisette felt happier than she had at any time since her mother's death.

This felt like home, she thought, idly reaching for the sponge and the tiny sliver of scented soap. It smelled of flowers, a soft aroma that grew as she lathered the sponge and then her body. She managed with only one hand until it became time to wash her hair. Reaching for the water that Giff had set close to the tub, she lifted it but could not figure out how to pour it over her head with only one hand. She struggled, splashing water onto the floor in the process and then smashed her injured hand between the bucket and the side of the tub.

"Oh," she moaned, leaning forward in the tub to cradle her hand. "Fiddlesticks!"

* * * *

Giff could taste her. Passion had heated her skin, dotting her flesh with the salty taste of her perspiration. Need had given her a luminescence that made her more exquisite to his eye than before. Her green eyes gleamed in the dim light of the loft as she lay under him, breathlessly begging him for more.

His hand cupped her breast, playing wickedly with the pale pink tip, watching it harden under his caress. She arched into him, her legs coming up to wrap around him, pulling him tighter to her, rubbing her sweet little cunny against the rock hard bulge of his cock.

"Tell me you want me," he growled. "Tell me you need me."

"I do," she whimpered. "Please."

Bending his head, he found the hard tip he'd been plying with his thumb, rolling the tip of his tongue around the taut bud. He flicked it gently before pulling it into his mouth and suckling, feeling her toes curl against the sides of his thighs. His hand slid down her flat little belly, his wide palm almost covering it.

"You're so tiny," he moaned around her nipple. "I don't want to hurt you."

"You won't," she said, shivering against him as his hot breath washed over her breast. "Please, make me yours."

"If I do, you aren't leaving here. You'll stay and be my wife."

"Oh," she cried out. "Fiddlesticks!"

"Fiddlesticks?"

He jerked awake, shaking his head as the dream didn't disperse right away. His hand slid across the bed, searching for the heat of her and found nothing. Then he heard it again. A frustrated moan came from below. He sat up, running his hands through his newly shorn hair. "Lisette?"

Grabbing a clean pair of drawers from his chest, he pulled them on and quietly went down the ladder, not wanting to wake his brothers. "Lisette?" he called again as he turned to face her, seeing her predicament right away. "Can I help?"

"It's not proper," she whispered, trying once more to lift the bucket and failing miserably.

"To hell with proper," he grouched. "You can't do this on your own, not with that burned hand. Sit forward."

She wrapped her arms around her knees, letting him have the bucket. He lifted it, pouring the warm water over her hair. Then he took up the sliver of soap she'd used on her body, lathering up his hands and slowly gathered her hair in them.

Lisette moaned softly as she felt his strong fingers in her hair, massaging her scalp as he washed it. It felt good, so much better than when her maid had done if for her when she was younger. It also seemed much more intimate, the two of them in front of the fire, him half dressed and her naked but for a tub of water.

Gifford felt his cock stiffen and wished for a pair of breeches. Touching her had an instant affect upon his body, making him ache with wanting. He took his time with her hair, washing it thoroughly, sliding his fingers around the small whorl of her ear, massaging her neck. He could tell she was enjoying his ministrations. Tiny moans and whimpers were dragged from her, each one going through him like a sensual jolt of electricity. With her hair full of suds, her back was exposed to his eyes completely and he couldn't help but follow the line of her spine down to where it disappeared into the water.

That was when he saw the marks. For a moment he thought his eyes were playing tricks on him. Maybe he was still sleep befuddled. He looked again and felt his anger rise until he wanted to roar in rage. Tamping it down wasn't easy though and he gritted his teeth, his finger moving down to just above the waterline, tracing the lash marks he could see.

She stiffened, and for a moment he thought she would jerk away from his touch. Then she relaxed, burying her face against her bent knee.

"Who did this to you?" he asked harshly.

She didn't answer, only shaking her head, mortified that he'd seen the marks of her step-mother's depravity.

"Lisette," he growled, moving on his knees until he could lift her chin with one finger. "Tell me who did that to you."

"It was my fault," she said suddenly, her eyes meeting his. "I was clumsy and too slow."

"I can't believe that," he growled. "You're as graceful as a doe."

"No, I wasn't good enough," she said miserably. "I broke a vase, spilled water across the rug and she cut her foot on one of the pieces of glass. She had to whip me."

"Who?" he urged. "Tell me who, Lisette. No one should whip someone as small and delicate as you."

"I…it was my stepmother." She blinked and a single tear slid down her cheek.

"Your father allowed this beating to happen?"

36

"No, he knew nothing about it. She made sure of that, and that he never saw what was happening to me." She reached up with her good hand, pushing soapy hair off her forehead. "Can you rinse this, please?"

"We are going to talk about this, Lisette. Your father needs to know what happened to you. Then he can do something about your step-mother." He picked up the bucket, pouring it with one strong hand while using the other to swipe the soapy water back from her face. Picking up the other bucket, he stood next to the tub, holding out his hand to her. "Stand," he said, swallowing hard at the thought of seeing her so close to him.

"B...but..." She sighed, taking his hand and letting him help her to stand. She stood before him, trembling not from the cold but from the feel of his eyes as they took in ever curve, every soft line of her naked body.

"God you're beautiful," he groaned, closing his eyes for a moment. His hand shook as he lifted the pail of warm water, his eyes meeting hers as he poured it over her trembling form. "How anyone could hurt you is beyond me."

When the water was gone and she was free of soap, he set down the pail. Instead of giving her his hand to help her out of the tub, he reached out, his hands sliding around her slender waist, lifting her easily out of the water to stand in front of the fire. Grabbing one of the towels, he stood before her. "May I?"

She nodded, unable to speak at the thought of his hands on her, even covered by the towel. Even his eyes, as they roamed over her body, felt like a heated caress upon her skin. It made her ache, and a strange feeling of yearning grew in her belly, twisting and coiling deep inside of her and he hadn't even touched her yet.

Giff started with her hair, dragging the heavy mass of off her shoulders and into the towel, squeezing the water from it gently. Wrapping the towel around her head, he reached for another, going to his knees in front of her.

She glistened in the light of the fireplace, the drops of water upon her skin glinting as the flames reflected from them. He watched, fascinated as one tiny drip slid from her collarbone, over the small swell of her breast, lingering for a single instant upon the tip before falling to the ground. Unable to stop himself, he leaned forward, gently kissing the soft pink nipple, then the other, wishing he dared to suckle them as he had in his dream.

She shivered and he pulled back, not wanting her to catch a chill. He patted dry her skin, starting at her neck and shoulders, carefully finding every drop of moisture on her skin. Her breasts moved with her quickened breaths, and he was hard pressed not to drop the towel to the floor and lick the rest of the drops from her body.

"Giff?"

"Yes," he whispered, looking up into her flushed face and seeing her heavily lidded eyes, gone hazy with desire.

"I feel... funny."

"Funny?"

"H...hot and...and shaky," she whispered, her hand going to his shoulder as he dried her breasts, his fingers moving across the hard tips with just the thin barrier of the towel between them. "My stomach feels... it aches."

He wanted to groan aloud at her words, but instead he forced himself to continue as he was, slowly making his way over her body. He heard her suck in her breath as he dried her slender belly, unable to resist stroking her skin with one finger. The satiny texture took his breath away, the sight of her soft mound covered with red/gold fleece made him yearn to discover her most secret flesh.

He moved to her legs, lifting one slender foot and then the other and drying them, then her ankles and calves, so sleek and slender. Her knees shook as his finger touched the back of them and she started to fall. He swept her up, standing, his eyes boring into hers. He could see desire, passion, need, all reflected to him in the emerald green of her eyes.

Lowering his head, he watched as her eyes fluttered shut, saw her lips part, her tongue peeping out to moisten the soft flesh. His eyes closed as he found her lips and felt the innocence of her response. She was sweet, her mouth pursed with a naiveté he found more arousing than the practiced kisses he'd experienced before.

The tip of his tongue touched her lips, brushed over the seam of them. Hers parted upon a gasp and he slipped inside, tasting of her passion as she timidly touched her tongue to his.

His groan was her reward, his hands slipping from her waist to run over the soft curve of her bottom, lifting her against him until she could feel his arousal pressing against the thin fabric of his drawers.

"I want you, Lisette," he growled against her lips. "If you don't want this, stop me now. I won't be able to stop later."

Her eyes flew open, staring into his. "I…I don't want you to stop," she said finally, the words rushing from her lips.

Her words sent a pulse of pleasure through him that was so strong he thought he'd lose control, coming in his drawers like some untried youth. He lifted her into his arms, moving to the sturdy table, laying her across its surface.

She looked like some divine feast spread out for his pleasure. For a moment, he could only stare at her in wonder, awed by her beauty and the gentleness of her spirit. Then she held her arms out to him, as eager for his embrace as he was for hers. He kissed her slowly, drawing her deeper into the passion that flared between them like a wildfire, their hearts racing out of control. She was a fast learner, quickly turning what he taught her and using it on him. Teeth, tongues, lips, all teased and tormented, tempted and tasted until she finally pulled away, out of breath.

"I…I didn't know I could feel like this," she groaned, arching into his searching hands.

"Your heart's pounding, Lisette," he said softly, his lips tracing the curve of her neck. "I can feel it, here," he said, his tongue lightly licking over her fluttering pulse. "And here." He traced his finger between her breasts, sliding it around the under curve of the slight mounds. "And even here," he whispered, sliding his body down until he sat in one of the chairs, his hands holding her thighs apart, tracing the wet pink flesh between.

"Oh, what are you doing?" she panted.

He smiled darkly, watching as his thumb pressed softly against her erect clit, stimulating that little bundle of nerves until she undulated against the table, her hands reaching for him. "I'm loving you."

"Oh God," she moaned, her whimpers turning into pleas. "S…Something's happening."

He leaned forward, replacing his thumb with his mouth, feeling her jerk as he sucked upon her clit, tasting her arousal upon his tongue. She cried out, muffling the sound with her hand, her body convulsing as she came. He lapped up her juices, even as her thighs squeezed around him.

Before she knew what was happening, he was between her legs once more, kissing her, letting her taste the sweet flavor of her arousal on his lips. His cock, freed from his drawers, was hot and hard between her thighs, resting against her wet slit. He held her hips, slowly moving against her, dragging the head of his cock over her sensitive clit over and over until she was breathless with what he made her feel.

"If I take you," he growled harshly in her ear, his breath hot against her skin. "I'm not going to let you go. We'll be sleeping together in my bed from now on. You'll be mine."

"I...I'll be yours?" Lisette asked, her eyes lambent with renewed desire. "Does that mean that you're mine?"

Giff smiled darkly. "Yes."

"Good," she said simply, lifting her head to capture his mouth.

He kissed her hard, the thought of her as his and his alone, making him almost desperate to take her. He had to restrain himself from plunging into her. She was so small, so delicate looking, and a virgin. He had to make to make this good for her.

Giff pulled away, standing in front of her. The head of his cock was wet with his own need as well as from her. He parted her lips gently, using his fist to aim his cock and then looked up at her. "I don't want to hurt you."

"Make me yours," she pleaded.

"Quick then, all right?"

She nodded eagerly.

One thrust did the deed, burying him halfway inside her tight sheath. He muffled her shriek with his mouth, forcing himself to be still inside her to let her get used to the feeling. His own body shivered as her heat enveloped him, the wetness caressing his throbbing cock. Giff fought the urging of his body to ride her fast and hard, to lose himself in the passion and pleasure of this act of love.

40

Lifting his head, he watched her face, seeing her white teeth gnawing upon her lower lip. "Are you all right?"

She nodded. "I feel so full."

"You aren't, not yet," he said, slowly pulling away only to push back inside, burying more of his hard cock into her quivering cunny.

She shivered under him, her hands coming up to hold onto his shoulders. He moved, cautiously at first and then harder, her moans of pleasure encouragement enough. Rocking against her, he reached down and lifted her legs onto his arms holding them in the crook of his elbows.

"Grab the table," he urged, pulling her hands down to grab the edge of the sturdy wood.

Long hard thrusts of his body made her writhe beneath him, quick jabs had her hips leaving the table, using the strength of his arms to rise up to meet him.

Her body grew taut under his, her eyes wild as she looked up at him. He could feel the first contractions that spoke of her climax around his hard flesh.

"Yes," he growled, his breath coming in hard pants. "Come for me, Lisette. Come on my cock."

A low moan came from her mouth and he slammed himself into her, throwing his head back and gritting his teeth as his own orgasm tore through him, enhanced by the feel of her cunny milking his cock. It seemed to go on forever as he spewed his seed into the beautiful girl beneath him.

Then he fell against her, his mouth finding hers. "You're mine now," he whispered against her lips.

"Yes," she whispered back. "And you're mine."

He felt her lips smiling under his and sighed. "Seems so."

He stood, pulling his still semi erect cock out of her. A gush of blood tinged semen escaped also. "We should get you cleaned up." He lifted her in his arms, moving so she stood in the still warm bath water. Picking up the rag she'd used, he soaped it again. "Hold onto my shoulders." When she did so, he lifted one of her feet and put it on the edge of the tub, opening her to his eyes.

His huge hands were gentle as they soaped her red, slightly raw looking flesh. "I'm sorry," he whispered as she flinched against his hand. "Does it hurt?"

"A little," she admitted, her skin rosy with her blushes as she let him perform this intimate task.

Cupping water in his hands, he washed away the soap then lifted her out of the tub once more, drying her gently with the towel, even going so far as to fluff the red curls on her mound. Then he handed her the nightgown she'd found in the trunk, pulling her still damp hair out from under the flat collar.

Giff blew out all the candles but one and led the way to the ladder.

"Oh no, the table," Lisette whispered, her hand to her mouth. "We forgot to wash it after…"

"…after we made love on it?" he asked, amused by her blushes.

"Yes," she said and he saw her set her slender shoulders. "We forgot to wash it after we made love on it."

"Go on up," he urged, smiling widely. "I'll take care of it."

She did as he bid, climbing into the huge bed. It was quiet in the loft, too quiet for the other two brothers to be sleeping. She knew they snored, it was one thing that had made her feel so safe the night before, letting her know she wasn't alone. Now her face blushed anew as she thought of them and what they might have heard, or, God forbid, have watched.

Gifford climbed into the loft, settling into the other side of the bed after blowing out his candle. He was naked, his drawers still on the floor where he'd taken them off earlier. He reached out, drawing Lisette against him.

"We'll start on an addition to the cottage," he whispered, just loud enough for her ears.

"An addition?"

"A bedroom for us," he answered. "Then you won't have to worry about what my dunderhead brothers might have seen." The last was said loud enough for the other two to hear and he heard Safford chuckle. "Now kiss me and go to sleep."

* * * *

Prince Rodbert rode at the head of a small formation of men. His standard flew above him, a white lion against a backdrop of sapphire blue. In the saddlebag, he carried the rolled scroll that had been signed by King Maxim. It made Lisette his and he planned on claiming her as soon as possible.

He was a tall man, but leanly built, that fact hidden by the armor he wore upon his person. His hair was so blonde as to almost be white, clubbed back from a face of almost feminine beauty. He had eyes the color of his standard, so blue that at times, they didn't seem real. Right now, they squinted in displeasure as they approached the castle gates.

"Atimas!" he called loudly, hearing the sound of his man's horse as it galloped up next to him.

"Yes, Highness?"

"Why has no one come to greet us or to even acknowledge our presence here?"

"They must be out searching for the Princess, Highness," Atimas said, trying to soothe the Prince's ruffled feathers. "Her father, King Maxim, is quite upset by her disappearance."

"This rudeness is intolerable, no matter the circumstance. Ride ahead and demand an audience with King Maxim." He waved the man off, watching as he galloped towards the castle.

He passed through the huge gates, his horse's hooves clattering over the stone that surrounded the courtyard. Only one man remained, standing slouched against the wall, his eyes half closed until he saw Atimas.

"Who goes there?" he said his voice quivering.

Atimas took a good look at the man. His hair was white, his skin wrinkled and pitted with scars. He was at least seventy, if he was a day. "They left you to guard the castle proper?"

"I may be old, lad, but there's still fight in these bones," the old man boasted. "What be your business here?"

"I am accompanying Prince Rodbert, Princess Lisette's intended. He has brought along men to help with the search. We wish to speak to King Maxim, immediately."

"He'll have to wait. King Maxim is out searching for his daughter."

"Then where is he searching, we shall go to him."

"I don't know. The king doesn't consult with the likes of me about his business. He rode off to the west, hours ago. If you wish to speak to someone, the queen is in residence." He huffed a sigh and then leaned back against the wall once more, his eyes on the man upon his horse.

Turning the horse, Atimas quickly galloped back to the prince, knowing the volatile young man was going to explode at being treated this way. "Highness, King Maxim is out searching for his daughter."

"But you told him that we would come, did you not."

"I did, Highness." Atimas bowed his head, waiting for the worst.

"Then I suppose we shall have to speak to the queen. Is she here, or did she leave to find her daughter also?"

Princess Lisette is Queen Edwina's stepdaughter, highness. King Maxim lost his first wife some time ago."

"Then she is here?"

"Yes, the queen is in residence," he said, repeating the old guard's words.

"Then make haste man, we've been riding for hours. I long for a drink and to get rid of the imprint of this saddle that is on my ass."

"You do not wish to join the search?" Atimas asked, though he already knew the answer. The Charmed Prince, as Rodbert was called, was actually spoiled and narcissistic, rarely willing to do anything that did not have a direct influence in making his life better.

The prince shrugged. "Who's to say she hasn't already been found and they are bringing the wayward child home now? If we were to go off in say…that direction," he waved his hand to the north, "she could be brought in from this direction, and then we've spent an entire day needlessly abusing our horseflesh." He sniffed, pulling a small handkerchief from the sleeve of his jerkin. "We shall wait for the King inside. Find food and shelter for the men and make my presence known to the queen."

"Yes, Highness," Atimas said, carefully keeping the loathing he felt for his ruler out of his eyes and voice. "It shall be as you wish."

* * * *

Queen Edwina paced her bedchamber, anxiously awaiting word from Geoffrey. She'd gathered all the supplies she needed to perform the magic necessary, transferring Lisette's youthful, winsome beauty to herself. The ritual would kill Princess Lisette leaving her with the small problem of removing the body. She shrugged; every plan had a detail or two that needed ironing out. With Geoffrey's help, getting rid of her body shouldn't be a problem.

A small scratching at her door had her jumping and hurrying over to open it. Instead of Geoffrey, she found a timid little maid, her eyes downcast, her body quivering in fear. "What is it?" she snapped.

"Prince Rodbert has arrived, ma'am, and is asking to see you," the maid managed to squeak out.

"Who?"

"He says he is Lisette's intended, Majesty." She squawked as Edwina grabbed her dress, hauling her up on her toes.

"What did you say?"

"P...Prince Rodbert claims to be Princess Lisette's intended," the girl squealed.

"And he wishes to speak to me? Why not to the King?"

"King Maxim hasn't returned yet, ma'am." She stepped back hurriedly when Edwina released her dress. Dropping a curtsey, she turned and scurried down the hallway, almost running by the time she got to the end.

"Prince Rodbert, eh?" she mused, tapping her fingers against her lips. She would have to send the man packing. Nothing could interfere with her plans for Lisette, not even a royal husband.

Hurrying to her mirror, she pinched her cheeks then smoothed the wrinkles from the silk dress she wore. The rose color of the gown gave her skin a youthful glow, she decided, and the neckline did wonders for the fullness of her breasts. She would do. Pasting on a cheery smile, she left her room.

* * * *

Morning came early in the little cottage and Lisette was up once more before the birds. She pulled on a shawl to cover the nightgown she'd worn to bed the night before, leaving Gifford sleeping peacefully and went down the ladder. Hurrying outside, she could see that the stars were beginning to lose their light as the sun started its sojourn across the sky.

Her trip to the privy made, she came back to the house, shivering at the chill in the air and the wet dew that had her toes curling. She set about straightening out the room, taking the bag of hair and stowing it away. It would be great to spread around her garden, when she planted one, to keep the wild animals away.

She picked up and deftly folded Gifford's drawers, glancing at the table with a sigh of satisfaction. Lovemaking had been wonderful, much better than anything she'd imagined before. Gifford had made her journey into becoming a woman a most pleasurable one. Remembering his promise to build them a room of her own, she couldn't help wondering what his intent was. But it didn't matter. She'd found a home her with her three gruff men.

"You look happy this morning," Safford said, sneaking up on her.

"Oh," she shrieked, jumping and then turned to slap at him as he laughed. "You shouldn't sneak up on a person so."

"I'm sorry," he said, hanging his head but a gleam of childish glee was in his eyes.

"Yes, like I'd believe that," she scoffed. She set Gifford's clothing down upon his chair, going and pulling the big pot and the kettle off their hooks to fill with water.

Safford took them from her. "You shouldn't be lifting with that hand yet, Lisette. You sit, I'll get the water started."

"I'll stoke the fire then," she said, wanting to do something.

"You just can't be still, can you, little one?" Safford chuckled, reaching out and caressing her cheek with friendly affection.

"Watch how you touch my woman, little brother," Gifford growled, sliding down the ladder. He came to her side, his fingers lifting her chin as his head bent, finding her lips for a kiss that was a little too long to be innocent. "Good morn, love," he said, lifting his head to see her eyes sparkling up at him. "Sleep well?"

"Yes, very well." She blushed when Safford snorted.

"You two should have slept like the dead from everything Mall and I heard." Safford ducked Gifford's halfhearted punch, going to the fire to stoke it, laying on the wood and then hanging the coffee pot over the burning logs. "Well, I don't think either of you were trying to be quiet about it," he grinned. "But we are definitely going to need that new room."

"Don't you ever get tired of listening in?" Giff asked, feeling his own cheeks heating.

"Weren't no listening in needed," Mall said, rubbing the sleep out of his eyes as he joined them. "We could have heard your caterwauling all the way at the mine."

"Would you two stop. You're embarrassing Lisette," Giff growled.

Lisette's shoulders were shaking and she'd buried her face in Giff's shoulder. He looked down, feeling her sobs against him.

"I'm going to kick the tomfoolery out of both of you," he snapped, rubbing his hands up and down Lisette's back. "Honey, don't cry. They don't mean nothing by what they say. They're just happy you're here."

"Oh damn, Lisette," Safford groaned, smacking himself in the head. "I ain't nothing but a dunderhead. Don't let my teasing upset you like this."

"You two done made her cry!" Mall exclaimed. "You should be ashamed."

Lisette lifted her face, bringing her shawl up to wipe at her streaming eyes. Her once silent laugher now enveloped the men, its charming sound startling all three. She tried to get control of her giggles but one look at the dumbfounded faces of her three men set her off all over again.

"She's laughing. Dammit all, Giff, she's laughing at us." Mallory sank down in the chair behind him, confounded by this mere slip of a girl who'd wormed her way into their lives.

"Dunderhead?" she giggled, letting her forehead rest against Gifford's chest.

"Find that funny, did you minx?" Giff drawled, his hands sliding from her back to dig his fingers into her sides, tickling her unmercifully.

"Stop!" she cried, laughing all the harder when he did. Her hand came up to his cheek, caressing his whiskered covered face. "Thank you," she managed to say when she got control of herself. "I haven't laughed like that in years, not since my father brought home his new wife."

"Good, now go fix us some breakfast, woman. Now that you're done with your shenanigans, we gotta get us to work."

* * * *

King Maxim rode into the castle grounds tired and hungry, but mostly, he was discouraged. He'd ridden for miles today, seeing no sign of anything that could have been Lisette's. Part of him wondered if she'd been kidnapped, stolen right out from under his nose, because he'd been too busy being King and not busy enough being a father.

He dismounted, handing over the reins of his mount to the stable boy. "Give him an extra measure of oats, he did good work today," he told the lad, giving his destrier one last pat.

The door of the keep proper stood open, firelight giving it a welcoming gleam. He walked up the steps, his thoughts on food and then sleep, so that he could be up at daybreak to search again.

The common room was full, strange men sitting and eating at his tables, drinking his ale and wine. He saw Edwina sitting at the King's table, her attentions on a blonde haired man. As he watched, she fawned over the man, allowing him glimpses of her tantalizing bosom, touching his arm and hand as they talked. He watched as the man threw his head back and laughed at something she said and knew a moment's jealousy.

But it quickly disappeared. How well Maxim knew of Edwina's charm and allure. He'd been the target of the same years before when he'd met her. She could put you at ease and make you believe you were the only man in her eyes before you could blink. He sighed. He wasn't sure what her scheme was now, but he knew it would have to do with this man.

"There he is," Edwina exclaimed, her hand resting upon the stranger's arm before sliding off. "Darling, we have guests and you weren't here to greet them."

"My daughter is missing, Edwina. Or did that small fact escape you again." He sighed heavily, forcing away the anger and exhaustion that was wearing him down. "I'm sorry for the outburst, sir. I have been in the saddle since before daybreak looking for my daughter."

"Then you must be tired and hungry," the man said generously. "The outburst is excusable under the circumstances."

He waited until Maxim had seated himself in his chair, the page behind it bringing him a warmed glass of mead and a platter of food. "I am Prince Rodbert, sir. I've brought my men to help with the search."

Maxim turned, startled. He'd forgotten about Rodbert and the contract he'd signed. "I'm speechless," he said finally, glancing around at all the men. "Thank you. They will come in very useful."

"Not at all. Lisette is my intended," Rodbert said slyly, reminding Maxim of the deal. "We shall be ready to leave before daybreak, sir." He stood, signaling to his men. "Might I wish you a good night, ma'am?"

Edwina extended her hand, feeling Rodbert take it in his own and lift it to his pretty lips. She smiled warmly at him, her eyes roaming over his exquisite features, features almost too delicate to belong to a man. "Good night, Prince Rodbert. I look forward to continuing our conversation soon."

"As do I, dear lady." Bowing low, he turned and left.

As soon as he disappeared, Edwina rose and saying not a word to her husband, made her way up the stairs towards her bedchamber. Maxim was left alone with his thoughts and his food before finding his own rest.

* * * *

Gifford kissed Lisette one last time before grabbing his shovel and hurrying after his brothers who had already disappeared from sight. She couldn't help but laugh, for he'd had trouble leaving her side, surprising even Mallory.

"Remember, stay inside and do not open the door to anyone," he called back as he left the clearing and hurried into the woods.

"He must think I'm two," Lisette mused, shaking her head, though she smiled at his caring.

Carrying the bowls to the sink, she clumsily did up the dishes and then climbed the ladder to the loft, making the beds and picking up the dirty clothes that seemed to always be there. A noise caught her attention and she went to the small window built in the front of the loft, startled to see two horses coming out of the woods, men upon their backs.

Fear sent her heart leaping into her throat and she hurriedly backed from the window, hoping that they hadn't seen here. She didn't recognize either man, but that meant nothing if Edwina had sent them out to look for her. A pounding on the door made her squeak and she searched for a hiding place.

"Open up!" a male voice shouted through the door. "We are here upon the King's business."

Chapter Four

Giff grinned as he hurried back down the trail from the mine, shaking the dirt out of his hair, and brushing his hands on his filthy pants. He'd been hard pressed to work the day, anxious to spend more time learning and loving his sweet little Lisette. She was his, he thought, every delicious inch of her.

He could almost hear her voice telling him that if she was his than it just made sense that he was hers too. Well, that was more than fine with him.

"There he goes," Safford chuckled, seeing his brother disappear around the bend in the trail.

"Yeah." Mall sighed, a lonely sound. "It just don't seem fair. I mean, I saw her first."

"What's it matter who saw who first, dimwit? Giff's the oldest. He should be first to find hisself a bride. You'll get your turn." Safford pushed his little brother, forcing him to pick up his feet and move down the trail. "Come on, I can't wait to find out what Lisette made for supper."

"You think with your stomach, Saff."

"Well, that's better than the part your thinking with, Mall," Saff crowed.

Mall dropped his pickaxe onto the trail, turning with his fists clenched. "You saying I'm thinking with my little head?" he growled.

"Yeah, so what's it to you?"

Mall grinned, swinging one huge, ham-like fist at his brother who dropped his hoe and ducked under the blow.

"You can't beat me Mall, you know that."

"Sure do, but it's a hell of a lot of fun trying." They scuffled, finally falling to the ground of the trail and rolling around in the dirt.

Saff planted his fist in Mall's gut, only to shake his head as Mall's fist caught him in the eye, making him see stars. He raised his fist, meaning to return the pleasure when Mall lifted his head, cocking it as if listening. "What's that?"

"What's what? I don't hear nothing."

"Shut up, Saff. It's Giff." They sprang to their feet, snatching up their tools as they ran towards the cottage. Giff's voice growing louder the closer they came to the clearing.

"Giff, what you making all that racket for?" Mall panted as he rounded the bend in the trail and stepped into the clearing.

"Lisette's gone, the place's been torn apart and she's gone." He sank down to his knees outside the door of the cottage. "Someone came here and took her from me."

Saff ran into the cottage while Mall got Giff to his feet. "That don't make no sense. Why would someone want to take her away?"

"I shoulda stayed here today," Giff growled, dropping his head in his hands. "I don't know where she's gone or who's taken her."

"He's right," Saff said, coming to the door of the cottage. "She put up quite a fight before they took her, there's blood in there."

"She could be hurt," Giff groaned.

"Excuse me, my dear fellows."

All three brothers whirled around, their hands coming up defensively.

"Oh, I didn't mean to alarm you," the man upon the horse said, drawing closer to the three men.

"Who are you, stranger, and what do you want?" Saff asked, stepping in front of his brothers.

"I come from the kingdom of King Maxim. We are searching for Princess Lisette. You by chance haven't seen her?"

"*Princess* Lisette?" Giff exclaimed, staring up at the fancily dressed knight on his huge destrier.

"Yes, have you seen her?"

"No," Mall said quickly. "She comes from that castle west of here?"

"Yes, that is the home of Maxim and his family. He's been searching for her since she disappeared days ago."

"We ain't seen hide nor hair of any Princess," Saff echoed his brother, wanting the knight to leave quickly.

"If you do see her, there is a reward offered for her safe return. The king is offering one hundred gold pieces," he said, his eyes taking in the small cottage and the dirty men. Then the knight bowed his head in a courtly manner, turning his horse he left the clearing.

"Did you see the look he gave us, Saff?" Mall asked, his eyes following the stranger as he made his way back out of the clearing.

"Stuck up sort," Saff growled.

"Princess," Giff whispered. "She's a princess. What's she want with a no account like me? She has ball gowns and carriages, and fancy knights bringing her gifts."

"Gifford, Lisette loves you," Safford grabbed his arms, giving his older brother a quick shake. "She gave you her virginity, didn't she? She didn't give that to no knight bringing her presents. So now, what we got to do is get you all fancied up like that knight there. Then you can go visit her and woo her proper."

"Besides, Giff, you saw the cottage, you saw what they did in there. Do you think she went peaceably like? She didn't want to go with them, not at all." Mall cocked his head. "I think it's time."

Safford nodded. "Yep, me too. We don't got to use all of it, but I think we need to sell off some of them. It's a good reason, Giff. You know it. Momma told us to save up for a rainy day, well I think it's storming."

Gifford looked back and forth between his brothers. Finally he nodded, reaching into the front pocket of his breeches and pulling out a ring of keys. Picking the right one, he handed it to Safford. "Only a couple. We don't want the secret getting out none."

Safford took the key as if he were being entrusted with the Crown Jewels. He held it delicately between his fingers before glancing over at Mall. The two of them turned, walking around the cottage and to the small outhouse behind it.

Both men looked around furtively before opening the door of the outhouse and stepping inside. The small building had been built against the hill at the back of their property. Saff found the small knothole in the wooden back and dug his nail in, popping the wood out and exposing a small keyhole.

"Ready?" he asked Mall.

"Yeah. Just do it already."

Saff rolled his eyes. Mall never had been one of ceremony. Then he slid the key into the keyhole turning it until it clicked. He pushed against the panel, feeling it give and then stepped into the small cave behind it. Mall was right behind him, pushing the hidden door open further.

Saff stuffed the keys in his pocket, grabbing one of the torches they kept close to the door and the box of matches kept on a shelf above them. He lit the torch, handing it to Mall and then another for himself before starting into the cave itself.

"How much you think we're going to need, Saff?"

"I'm thinking to do this up right, we might want two of the big ones."

"Two?" his little brother asked. "Well, how we going to explain two?"

"Same way we always do," Saff said. "Come on, Mall. We gotta get that little girl back for Giff. They need each other."

They turned into another room in the cave and stopped, looking around. The light from their torches shone on the treasure within, gems mined from their mine, were stockpiled in the cave. Casks and boxes, crates and chests filled with the multicolored stones were piled everywhere. Saff stepped into the room, going to a crate in the corner. Reaching in, he easily picked out the stone he wanted.

A fiery red ruby winked in his palm, cut by Mall, the gem was about as large around as a robin's egg. "You did good with this one, Mall. It's pretty."

Mall walked past, shrugging his big shoulders at the compliment. "Yeah, it passes the time when the veins ain't playing out. What about this one?" he asked, reaching down and lifting a pale blue sapphire. It wasn't as big as the ruby but the color was unusual and the cut was exquisite.

"Naw, I was thinking more along the lines of one of them sapphires, the dark blues ones." Saff lifted a much smaller stone from the rest, letting it glint in his palm as Mall picked out one of the sapphires. It was a square cut emerald, a perfect size for a ring. It winked green fire in his hand until he closed his fist around it and shoved it in the front pocket of his pants.

"What you going to do with that?"

"Every bride needs a ring," Saff said. Turning, they left the gem cave without a glance back at all the beauty of the cut and uncut stones that lay in its depths, going back to the front of the cave and extinguishing the torches. Mall went through the hidden door first while Saff dug out the keys, closing and locking it behind him and replacing the fake knot in the wood.

Giff was still sitting where they'd left him, staring around hopelessly. "It ain't going to work," he groaned, dropping his head in his hand. "I ain't ever going to be spiffed up enough to make them think I'm some kind of Prince or gentleman. I should just face facts. Lisette's gone."

Mall reached down, lifting Giff to his feet by a handful of shirt. Staring at him for just a moment, he hauled back and let his fist fly, hitting his square in the cheek with a punch that would have put a lesser man down for the count.

"What the fuck you do that for?" Giff growled, his hands coming up to fist in front of him.

"My big brother don't whine and moan like some woman about piddly shit that don't mean nothing anyhow. You said Lisette loves you and you love her, right?" Mall asked, waiting until Giff nodded his head. "Then quit fucking feeling sorry for yourself and let's go get her back!"

Saff walked up next to them both, chuckling. "Little brother, you talk better with your fists than any man I know." He grabbed Giff's arm. "Come on, man. We got miles to go before dark. We'd better get cleaned up and get at it."

"Yeah," Giff said slowly, his eyes losing their hopeless expression. They took on a glint of determination that even the slowly forming welt around them couldn't deny. "Let's go."

* * * *

Lisette struggled furiously between the two men who were escorting her into the castle. "Let me go!" she screamed, kicking out her feet. Her heel connected sharply with one man's shin, causing the man to snarl and limp a step. He already looked worse for wear with his clothing torn by her sharp nails, scratches racked down the side of his face and onto his neck. He wore the impression of her teeth in his ear and the marks of her fists everywhere else.

He was the one that got off lightly. The other man could barely walk from the bruising impact of Lisette's knee in a certain sensitive area of the male anatomy. When he spoke, his voice squeaked the first few syllables until he'd clear it to make it return to normal. His hand was swollen from where this tiny princess had slammed it in the door and he had scratches and bite marks from his attempt to put her over his shoulder that he wouldn't show anyone.

If it hadn't been for the fact that she was King Maxim's daughter, he'd have locked her in that cottage and lit it on fire, burning her as the witch he thought she was. Instead, he held up his part, carting her royal carcass into the great room, eager to dump her upon her father and walk away to lick his wounds.

"Lisette?"

Both guards sighed in relief at hearing the queen's voice. "We've found her, Highness."

"She is unhurt?"

"Yes," squeaked the second guard before clearing his voice. "She was in an old cottage in the woods."

"What happened to you two men? Were you attacked?"

They looked at each other, dropping Lisette's arms. "She wasn't pleased to see us, ma'am."

"I would say. Have the healer check your wounds and bind them. I will inform King Maxim of your return and that you bring us back our lost daughter. Go, I shall escort her to the King."

"I am not your daughter," Lisette said, her voice low, her heart pounding violently in her chest. She was terrified because she knew the Queen would not take her to her father.

"No, and good thing, I'd have drowned you at birth," Edwina hissed, grabbing Lisette's arm in a tight grip. "You've led me on a merry chase, Lisette. Now that it's over, would you care to know what your father planned for you?" Without waiting for the girl to answer, she pushed on a square of wall just off the stairway, watching as it swung inward then pulled Lisette inside with her. "Be quiet and learn of your father's perfidy."

Lisette's curiosity won out and she clamped her mouth closed. Following the Queen was not an issue for the woman refused to let go of her arm, dragging Lisette along behind her.

She stopped behind a latticed wall, pointing through the small holes. "Look and listen."

Lisette stared at her father for she could not recall seeing him look as upset and small as he did at this moment. "She is still missing, Prince Rodbert. I will not have her marriage to you done in proxy."

"King Maxim, on the contract that you signed, it states that if the Princess is not returned to her home within six days of my arrival here, the marriage will go ahead. A proxy with stand in for the Princess or else you will forfeit your kingdom and your crown... to me." Prince Rodbert smiled, his eyes narrowing as he spoke the last words. He strode to the dais upon which the king's throne sat, turning to eye the room critically.

It was the first that Lisette had seen the man and her heart leapt into her throat. He looked cruel and cold, with a bearing that was false in her eyes. This is the man her father had promised her to in marriage? She'd rather die.

"That can be arranged," the queen's hoarse whisper sounded in her ear. "I've already made arrangements. You will marry the Prince, but a tragic accident will befall the two of you as you leave the kingdom. His body will be found. Yours, on the other hand, will be swept away. Your father will pine for you and for the tragedy that he allowed to happen. He shall fall into his cups, drinking away his sorrows. Then, alas for Queen Edwina, he shall stumble down the stairs, breaking his fool neck, leaving her his only living heir and the ruling Queen here."

"No," Lisette whispered, her hand going to her lips as her stomach turned at the queen's treachery. "No, I won't allow it."

"You won't have any say. You'll be dead. But do not worry, my dear. Your death is for a good cause." She preened, pushing a loose pin securely back into her coiffure. "Now come, and make not a sound or I shall kill you now."

"You're evil," Lisette hissed.

"You're just realizing this now, my dear?" Edwina asked with a quiet chuckle. She dragged Lisette down the hidden corridor, climbing a flight of crooked stairs and then pushing through another doorway. This one led to her bedchamber.

Geoffrey stood inside, cleaning a bright red stain from his sword. "It has been done, majesty. They will not tell of finding the Princess."

"Good, Geoffrey. I always know I might count on you. When I am running this kingdom, you shall rule at my side." Edwina moved towards him, dragging the struggling Lisette easily along with her. She lifted her hand, stroking his face slowly, her eyes upon his. "Now, strip this wretched girl that I might prepare her for my spell."

Geoffrey took Lisette from Edwina, easily overpowering her. "Your tricks will not work upon me," he hissed at her, lifting her so that her heels beat ineffectually against his high boots. He pushed open another secret passage, this leading to a room behind the Queen's bedchamber. He started to close the door behind him, only to be stopped by Edwina.

"You might play with her if you like, Geoffrey, but she must remain a virgin for the spell will not work otherwise. I will return later, after I inform Maxim of his daughter's return and her illness."

"Yes, my love. It will be as you say." He let her touch his cheek once more, feeling a cold shiver creep up his spine at the feel of her wretched hands upon his skin.

She left and he closed the door, locking it securely with a heavy metal key that he hung upon a hook far above Lisette's head. He turned to the small Princess, his eyes sad, his shoulders slumping, knowing what was expected of him.

"If I do not do as she says, I will be next upon her list to kill," he said softly, watching as Lisette backed slowly away from him. "I do not wish to harm you, Princess. Please, forgive me."

Lisette watched with wary eyes as the tall man knelt before her, bowing his head, his anguish apparent. "Then why do you do this?" she cried. "Let me go, let me go back to Giff, please!"

Geoffrey flinched at the plea in her voice, the sound of her tears striking another chord in his chest. "I am damned," he whispered.

"No," Lisette shook her head, slowly creeping closer to the man. "Help me and I will protect you. My father will help you. Please, don't let her do this thing she has planned."

"You don't know what she is, what she will do," Geoffrey sighed, lifting his head to watch her come even closer. "I must obey her, Princess." He reached out, taking the hem of her borrowed dress in his hands and pressing his lips to it. Then he stood swiftly, reaching out and taking her into his arms, lifting her off the ground.

"No!" Lisette screamed, her nails going to his face.

He made no move to stop her, feeling the pain of her scratches as less than what was due him. He carried the struggling form easily to the stone slab that sat in the center of the room, laying her gently upon it and holding her there with one hand.

Her fist struck him hard, enough to make him flinch and blood to well from his mouth. He let it drip down his chin, watching as it fell upon the pale skin of her breast, trailing to form a small puddle between her breasts. "It is no more than what I deserve, Princess."

"You are mad!" she cried, watching as he made no move to avoid her blows, only flinching in pain as they landed upon his skin. His brown eyes met hers, the sadness she saw in them startling her. She stopped struggling, lifting her hand to his face.

"Why?" she asked softly, tears falling down her cheeks. "I had but one short moment of happiness and you tear it from me. Please," she begged, seeing his own tears fall from his eyes. "Please, let me go."

His hand trembled against her skin. "There is but one way that she will fail, Princess. If you are willing…"

"Anything," Lisette said quickly, grasping his hand in her own. She felt him pull away, his trembling fingers moving over her, rising to curve around the slight curve of her breast.

"Anything?" he asked, looking into her eyes so she knew the truth.

Her head shook, the negative coming to her lips as the horror of what he was saying sank in. "You're mad."

"Her spell will not work if you are no longer pure, Princess. Give yourself to me and I will save you." He bent his head, his other hand coming up to her face and forcing her head to still, clamping on her jaw so that he might find her lips.

His mouth was hot, his breath heavy as it hissed against her skin. His lips and then his tongue muffled her protests, as he drove it into her mouth. He moved over her, holding her down now, easily grabbing her wrists with one hand while with the other, he jerked on the front of her gown.

She felt his hand on the bare curve of her breast, his thumb brushing with insistence against the soft pink tip. She squirmed against him, desperate to tell him no, to scream that she'd given herself to the man she loved. But he gave her no chance, ripping at her clothes like a starving animal.

His mouth left hers, dropping to her breast and she felt the heat of his mouth suckling hungrily upon her breast. His weight held her down, his cock an impatient presence against her leg, pressed with relentless tenacity.

"Stop!" she sobbed. "Please, don't do this. I'm not a virgin!" she cried, her body arching as she tried to throw him off of her.

"You lie," he growled, his eyes hot and hungry, his mouth a mere breathe from her nipple that shone with the saliva he'd left upon it. "You will not save yourself with lies."

"It is not a lie," she groaned, shivering as her nipple tightened in the contrast of cold air after his hot mouth. "I gave my virtue to the man I love."

He seemed to consider this even as his tongue lapped out to play with the taut tender bud, flicking it and curling around it to draw it into his mouth once more. Humming his pleasure with the sweet treat, he cocked his head to the side, biting gently and stretching the bud until it was almost painful before letting go to watch her breast jiggle.

"If that is true, than what matters one more?" he asked. "You are beautiful, Lisette. Your taste is better than the most flavorful of foods. If you are no longer virginal, than one more between your thighs will give you no pause."

She shook her head, staring at him in horror. "No, please. I do not love you. I do not want you to do this."

He dropped his head, nuzzling his nose around her wet nipple, breathing in her scent. "I can smell your arousal, Lisette. You are not unaffected by what I do."

"No," she moaned. "It is not true. I love but one man. Only he may possess my body."

"We shall see. First I must discern if you lie or not about the state of your innocence. He smiled at her, his grin one of lascivious pleasure. His hand slid down her stomach, cupping the soft mound of her cunny through the fabric of her dress and petticoat before moving further. He traced the line of her legs, forcing his hand between until he reached her knees. Then he grabbed her skirt, pulling it up, baring her slowly to his eager gaze.

"You have beautiful legs, Lisette. I can scarcely wait to feel them clasping my rutting hips as I take you." His palm moved up her soft inner thighs, forcing apart her legs, holding them apart with one of his own. She cringed as she felt his thumb brush against her swollen lips and the soft curls that covered her mound, crying out once more for him to stop.

"Please, no! No...I...I'd rather die," she sobbed, straining to close her slender thighs.

"Ah," he grinned. "Then you do lie about your innocence."

She shook her head, her hair flying around her face, tangling in the wetness from her tears, blinding her. "N...no!" It was all that she could think to say, all that came to her tortured mind as her tender muscles foiled her attempt to thwart his rape as he pulled her legs wide apart.

"Such beauty," he mused to himself. "Such tender sweetness hidden between the delicate stems of your legs, Lisette. You should be proud of this, of the lovely pink flesh you try so very hard to hide from me and the rest of us men." His fingers slid into the wetness of her slit, toying with her, enjoying her scent and her heat after making love to the cold body of the queen. He found the tiny pearled nub at the top of her valley, rubbing his finger around and against it and feeling her jerk in reaction.

Looking into her face, he smiled at the wildness of her eyes, the way her breathe seemed to catch as if she couldn't fill her lungs. Her pupils dilated, almost hiding the intense green of her irises. She closed her eyes as he watched, turning her head to the side, sobs shaking her slender body.

"Your tears matter not, Lisette. I will take you and then we will flee this place. We will go where the queen cannot find us." He slid his fingers down her wetness, his thick middle digit finding the passage of her sex, teasing the opening as if afraid to find out the truth of her words.

As he began to push into her, stretching the delicate tissues that had known only Giff's hand, she screamed her denial, the sound echoing throughout the chamber, almost seeming to mock her.

"Stop!"

* * * *

Giff could barely stand still as the tailor measured and fitted new clothing to his tall, wide frame. He growled at the man, making him cringe and drop his pins before Safford could step in to calm his brother.

"The more you fidget the longer it takes. Hold still, Giff, and let the man do his business." His clothing had already been fitted, Mall standing beside another man and holding his arms out at the man's insistence.

"I don't see why we got to get gussied up too. It's Giff that's planning on taking the vows, not us, Saff."

"Shut up your fussing. It's not often we get to go to court. Who knows, maybe you'll meet the girl of your dreams while we're helping Giff retrieve his." Saff walked between his two brothers wishing he could just knock their heads together and get it done with.

The bell over the door of the fancy shop that had been their second stop on their way to the castle, jingled lightly, announcing the arrival of a new customer. Saff glanced up, his eyes lighting on the woman who entered for only a moment before he went back to his pacing. He'd made only half a circuit before his body stopped as if struck by lightning. His head turned slowly and he watched as the young woman and another older woman walked toward a row of bolts of material. "Oh, holy mother in heaven," he breathed, almost struck dumb by her.

"Miss Giselle," the man squawked that was fitting Mall. "I have your order ready if you can wait but one moment."

The vision turned, her eyes landing upon Safford for one instant before dismissing him as unimportant. "A very short one, if you please. I have other matters to deal upon while I am about today."

Her voice was musical, matching her beauty. Brunette and tiny, her head would barely come to Safford's wide chest. The diminutive lady was dressed beyond pall in a gorgeous creation of pale purple silk that showed off her tiny waist and bountiful breasts. Her lips were full, the upper one a touch bigger than the lower, giving her an unusual look, her eyes were a shade darker than her gown, a color not seen often and never by the beauty-stricken Safford. He found his feet moving before he realized what he was doing and suddenly he was in front of her. His mouth opened but not a word came out.

"Yes?" Giselle asked, her tone irate for the man was big and dirty, his face streaked with grease or soil. "Did you wish to say something?"

Her tone snapped Safford out of his spell. He stuck his big hand out. "Hi, I'm Safford."

The girl took one look at his gigantic hand and the dirt encrusted nails and shuddered. "I'm sorry," she said, her nose going into the air. "You've obviously mistaken me for someone else." She turned, rolling her eyes when she caught the gaze of her companion.

"Well, you don't have to be rude about it, Missy," Saff growled.

"Rude? Excuse me, sir, but you began with rudeness. You don't accost females without getting the permission of their guardians. Not to mention your hygiene is definitely lacking. Now excuse me," she snapped, turning her back on Safford.

His hand came out before he realized what he planned to do. He grabbed her arm, spinning her back around and pulling her into his arms. "You need a lesson in manners," he growled, his arm lifting her so that he could easily reach her lips. He kissed her hard, that unusual mouth of hers sending his desires spinning. Then he dropped her to her feet, turned and, without another word, walked away from her.

"Well," she gasped when she could speak again. "I never…"

"Yeah," he called back. "It shows. Your kissing could use some work, girl. When you want to practice, look me up." He walked up to Giff who just stared at him as if he were completely crazy. "I'm going to marry her," he whispered, smiling hugely.

Chapter Five

Lisette's screams were muffled, her body writhing and squirming under Geoffrey's. She could feel his fingers against her most intimate flesh, feel him pushing inside of her, his breathing hard and harsh against her skin.

The door slammed open, the lock clacking to the floor. Prince Rodbert stood there, his sword in hand. "Release her," he growled.

Geoffrey rose to his feet, standing before the man, his hand behind him, motioning for Lisette to stay where she was. "You only want to hurt her, Rodbert. You care not for her feelings."

"You stand and speak of feelings when you were raping her?" Rodbert stepped into the room, his sword swishing in front of him. "Draw your weapon, man. We will settle this as gentleman."

Lisette rolled away from Geoffrey, holding her torn gown closed with her hands. "No..." she moaned, moving away from both men.

"Princess Lisette, you are safe," Rodbert said, holding his hand out to the brutalized girl.

She stared at him, unwilling to trust either man.

"Lisette!"

She turned, seeing her father rush into the room. "Oh," she cried, running into his open arms. "Father..."

"No, it's all right now. We will talk when we get you out of here. Take him into custody," Maxim growled, sending his guard forward to grab Geoffrey. "I want him in the dungeon. I'll decide what to do with him later."

"No..." Geoffrey began, his eyes flashing to Lisette's face. "She'll kill me, Lisette. Please, you can't let her get away with this."

"Father..." Lisette lifted her head, her eyes locking onto Geoffrey's. "He'll be in danger."

"Why should you care? The monster tried to rape you."

"But in his own confused way, he was trying to save me."

"Save you from whom?" Rodbert said, coming close to the beautiful red haired maiden he'd contracted to marry.

64

She stared at him, a feeling of shyness and fear keeping her lips closed. Her eyes dropped and she stared at her father's chest, unable to speak.

"Lisette?" Maxim questioned, his voice urging her to speak. "Who did he think to save you from?"

"Her, father. My s…stepmother."

"Edwina?" His voice might have sounded disbelieving, but in his heart he knew she spoke the truth. "What reason would she have to harm you, daughter?"

"It was for a spell!" Geoffrey cried, fighting the men who held his arms so tightly. "She was going to kill Lisette so that she would have ever lasting youth and beauty!" He jerked forward then back, pulling free. "I won't let her kill me!" he screamed, running through the doorway and into the other room. A shrill and eerie shriek followed, seeming to echo upon the air as King Maxim's men hurried after him, stopping when they saw what waited in the Queen's chamber.

Lisette felt her blood freeze at the sight of Geoffrey, his body laid out on the floor like a doll forgotten and discarded during play. It wasn't the sight of his body that had her afraid, though, but the way his head lay. Somehow it had been turned all the way around, his neck twisted so that, though his body faced away, his head was tilted toward her, his wide open eyes filled with the horror of the last thing visited upon him.

"No," she whispered.

"What could have done this?" Maxim cried, holding Lisette closer.

"Your wife," she said, turning to look up into his eyes. "Father, she is evil. Please, let me go back to where I was before."

"You are to be my wife, Lisette. I will protect you from any threat." Rodbert stepped up, holding his hand out to Lisette.

"I don't even know you," she whispered, staring at his hand and remembering his words to her father.

"We shall become more acquainted, my dear. Most royals never meet their intended before the wedding." He smiled though it didn't reach the blue of his eyes.

"Father," she cried, turning to Maxim with fear in her eyes. "I do not want to marry this man."

Maxim sighed. "I've signed the contract, Lisette. Only Rodbert can break the pact."

"And that is something I have no plans of doing. You shall grow to love me in time, Lisette, just as I shall you. I am a kind and fair man and I can be very generous." He smiled wider, reaching for her arm. "Come now, we must make ready to leave this place."

"No! I am not going with you." She grabbed Maxim's arm, turning her back on Rodbert.

"Such virginal shyness can be excused a first time, Lisette. Do not try my patience anymore. Your father knows what is involved and what he would lose if you refuse my suit." Rodbert wrapped his hard, cruel fingers around her slender arm, yanking her away from Maxim hard enough that her hands slipped off the material of her gown, exposing her breast.

"Stop! Please," she cried.

"Tell her Maxim," Rodbert said, his eyes on the smooth, soft globe that lay exposed to his eyes. "You are very beautiful, Lisette, but I prefer my wife to show a modicum of decorum in her dress and actions." He reached up, pulling the two torn edges together over her breast, his little finger rubbing against her nipple and lingering, making his actions very obvious.

She tried to jerk away, resulting in ripping the old gown more. "You are no gentleman," she hissed.

"I never claimed to be," he whispered, holding her close enough that she could feel the heat of his breath against her face. "Now, go to your chamber, dress yourself as befitting a princess, and then come to the great hall. We shall eat and then discuss the marriage plans."

* * * *

Lisette shook as she reached her chamber door, the guard Rodbert had sent with her, following silently behind her. Opening the door, she shivered, remembering the day she'd runaway. She'd never even had a chance to stop at her chamber. The room was destroyed; even the mattress upon her bed was torn apart, ripped open by some sharp instrument. Her gowns were strewn over the room like a brightly colored carpet, some ripped, others wadded into balls. The portrait she had of her mother was lying in the cold fireplace, covered in soot.

Her hand over her mouth, she knelt next to the unlit hearth, reaching in and pulling out the portrait. Tears ran down her cheeks as she tried to brush the grim from the painted face, only resulting in smearing it across the brush strokes. "Mama," she whispered. "I'm so sorry."

She took the picture to where it used to hang. Putting it back, she looked around the room, wanting to sit down and cry. "Gifford," she sighed heavily. "Where are you?"

* * * *

Giff pulled on the tight collar of the shirt that had just been delivered to the small tavern/inn that he and his brothers were staying at. "This will never work," he growled at Safford. "I look foolish."

"You look like a man intending to court his lady," Saff said, hearing the same words that Giff had been spouting for the past hour. "You can't go to King Maxim and ask for his daughter's hand wearing the dirty work clothes you had on."

"I'm not a Prince or even a lord. How could he even consider me for his daughter?" He dropped his hands into his head, feeling hopeless.

"You have something none of them have," Mall chimed in. "You have Lisette's love. If King Maxim is the kind of man I think he is, he will want his daughter's happiness over some title."

Gifford sighed, reaching out to snag the leather jerkin. "I hope so," he groaned.

Saff turned from looking out the shuttered glassless window. "Let's go," he urged.

"You just want to see if you can find your prickly lady," Mall accused.

The three brothers looked completely different from when they'd entered the inn. After baths and shaves, wearing new clothing and new boots, they climbed down the narrow stairs. Mall's eyes lingered on the sassy little barmaid that was serving the few customers in the tavern, smiling as she gave him a wink, walking away with a little extra wiggle to her hips.

"She's not for you, lad," Giff said, slapping him on the shoulder.

"And why not?" Mall asked, glaring at his older brother.

"She'd take your money and ride you just fine but then, she'd probably rob you blind." Saff grabbed his shoulder, squeezing it. "Come on, let's go get Lisette back and then you can go see if you can find a filly to fulfill your needs."

"I still find it hard to believe that we had a Princess cooking us food and cleaning our cottage," Mall laughed. "She sure didn't look like any Princess I've ever seen before."

"How many Princesses have you seen?" Giff asked.

Mall just shrugged, pushing open the outside door and stepping out into the evening air. The sky was rosy, the encroaching night hanging just beyond the touch of the lowering sun. The first evening star could be seen at the very edge of the horizon in the east, dull in the view of the sun's glorious setting colors. Birds sang their good nights from the branches of trees, occasionally swooping to catch a last insect before settling for the night. The men made their way to the castle, slipping past guards with nary a single command to halt them. Walking up the wide steps to the huge doorway in the courtyard, Gifford grew more worried, for it shouldn't have been so easy to enter a castle as well guarded as this.

"Why haven't we been stopped?" he hissed to Safford.

"I was wondering the same," his brother replied, showing his nervous demeanor as he glanced around at the guards nearby. Not a soul was watching them or gave them more than a single look. "Something is wrong."

* * * *

Lisette dressed in the least wrinkled gown she could find, the linen underskirt feeling coarse against her skin after wearing the worn dresses that Gifford had provided her with. She brushed out her hair, pinning it back up and draping a soft snood over it. After washing her face and hands with cool water, there was nothing more she could do in the destroyed room. Her steps were slow, her eyes showing her dread as she made her way towards her father and the man he'd contracted her to marry. What she longed to do was to flee this place once more, to run back to Gifford and the strength of his arms, feel his lips once more, his body against her own. She glanced back at the men following her, their eyes never leaving her person and sighed.

She would get nowhere with these two stalking her every move. She had to find a way to be rid of them.

She made it down the last few steps and into the great room, seeing more men than usual gathered at the tables to enjoy the evening repast. Her father sat in his place of honor, though he wore a frown upon his usually agreeable face and his eyes met hers and then slid away. It alarmed Lisette more that he wouldn't meet her eyes and she felt a pang of fear.

"There is my bride-to-be," Prince Rodbert exclaimed, coming up to meet her. He lifted her cold hand in his own, brushing a kiss along her knuckle before twining it through his arm.

Lisette badly wanted to pull away, but felt the eyes of all gathered upon her, watching as she was almost ceremoniously led to where her father was seated. "What is this?"

"I felt no need to wait, my dear. We have the priest and all the witnesses needed to make our joining legal in the eyes of God and man. Then, as soon as it is done, we shall depart for my…er…our home." He patted her hand, clamping down upon it as he felt her begin to struggle. "If you refuse, your father will lose his crown and be banished and I shall rule this land as well as my own. Then I shall make you my mistress instead of my wife. It is your choice, Lisette?"

"But…" Her mouth closed for she knew there was nothing she could say that would dissuade him from this course he'd set. Inside, she cried out for the love she'd known from Gifford, wondering if he would even miss her or even cared that she'd been taken. "What of my step-mother?" she cried, grasping at any straw that would put off this sham of a marriage.

"She is no threat, Lisette. What is one woman against a man of my power?" He preened, looking for all the world like a silly peacock strutting about and showing off his plumage.

"Sir Geoffrey felt differently."

His eyes narrowed at her words and he halted his steps, turning her to face him. "Geoffrey was a rapist and a murderer. Perhaps you felt more for him than you originally let on?"

"No," she hurried to say, seeing the threat before her. "I only know what he said to me during that time before you broke down the door. He feared that she is a witch. She even spoke to me of spells and such during that time, saying she would marry me to you and then kill you before you could…you could…" She ducked her head, knowing she'd said too much.

"Before I could make you mine in body as well as in name?" he asked, his hand tightening even more upon hers.

Lisette gasped as he squeezed her flesh hard, her fingers turning white under his grip. "Please, sir," she cried. "You're hurting me!"

His eyes gleamed as if enjoying her pain, then they cleared and he released the grip upon her fingers though he didn't allow her to move away from him. "We marry now," he declared loudly so that all could hear. "Then we will leave for my kingdom with the King's blessing."

Maxim looked up, his eyes sadly taking in his daughter, turning from her hopeful expression. There was naught he could do to retain his kingdom. He comforted himself with the thought that Lisette would have been married off at some time or another. Now was just as good as then. His eyes took in the empty chair next to his own, the chair his wife, Queen Edwina, had always occupied. Now if she were found, she would be questioned as a heretic and most likely burned as a witch.

"You are going to give us your blessings, are you not, King Maxim?" Rodbert said, stepping up in front of the King and bowing.

"Y…Yes, of course I am. You will make him a good wife, Lisette. Be true and dutiful and fulfill his wishes and I am sure you will be happy, my daughter." He tried to hide the doubt in his tone by smiling widely, failing miserably in the effort.

"Do you wish to give the bride away, Highness?" Rodbert asked, though he refused to release her arm.

Instead, he waved forward the priest, forcing Lisette to her knees beside him and bowing his head.

The ceremony was short, the moment when Lisette was forced to recite her vows came and she stared up at her father, wishing for some sign from him that what was happening was against his wishes. When none was forthcoming, she said her "I do" in a timid voice, feeling tears streak down her cheeks.

Finally it was done, Rodbert leaning toward her and placing a chaste kiss upon the side of her mouth. "It is done, wife. Now, we must face our people and you must smile and play the happy bride." He smiled grimly as she merely stared at him. "That wasn't a request my dear. Make them believe you are happy, or you will pay for it later."

Lisette felt a chill of fear creep up her spine. She forced a smile upon her face, though it was sickly at best. Turning, she felt his arm come up around her, pulling her in close to the heat of his body. Her eyes swam over the crowd of men and women, all laughing and shouting, yelling in their enthusiasm at the impromptu wedding. Then her eyes met those of the man who'd walked in the door. Brown eyes, once so warm and sweet, glared at her with a coldness that sent a shiver of dread through her. His face was hard, his mouth set in an expression of rage. He struggled in the hold of his brothers, as she watched, he stood as if frozen; then turned, leaving the hall.

"Gifford," she whispered miserably.

"What? Did you speak, wife?"

"N...no," she sighed, swallowing the sobs that wanted to erupt from her, blinking back the tears that ached to be shed.

* * * *

Toasts were made and drank to, congratulations given and received. Lisette huddled in the chair she'd been placed in, barely raising her eyes, afraid that she would once more see Gifford staring at her with hatred in his eyes. She spoke when spoken to and ate what was put in front of her, though she neither tasted nor wanted the food. It was almost a relief when Rodbert pulled her from her chair, bidding her to wish her father farewell, for they were leaving this night to return to his home.

"She should be allowed her wedding night in a bed," Maxim argued, though with little heat.

"Whether it is a bed or the seat of a coach, have no fear, your daughter will be well compensated," Rodbert jested, sending all within earshot to laughing.

Maxim flushed, his anger palpable. "She is my daughter, sir."

"She is my wife, Maxim. I will be deciding her fate from now on."

"Do not," Lisette begged her father. "It is done, I have no choice. Just let it be, Father."

"I hate what my desperation has caused, Lisette." Maxim began to say more but she held up her hand, going into his arms and pressing her lips against his cheek.

"I shall miss you, Father. Be safe," she whispered.

His arms tightened, drawing her near before he released her reluctantly. "And you," he said softly.

"Come, Lisette. The coach is ready and waiting."

"But...I have not packed," she cried, following him as he held onto her hand.

"Your needs shall be met, wife. Tis all you need to know."

He dragged her out the door and down the wide stairs, grasping her around the waist as he lifted her into his coach. Her skirts were barely inside before he gave last instructions to the driver. Then he closed the doors behind himself, making sure that the locks were firmly in place.

The horses were off as soon as he'd settled into the seat across from her, his eyes making Lisette very nervous. They roamed her slim frame, seeming to strip her bare of the gown she'd worn for her impromptu wedding. Her hands fluttered upon her lap, coming up to clutch at her throat, as if she could protect what little innocence she had left.

"You look as if you expect me to pounce," he chuckled, laughing at the fear he could see in her eyes.

"Is that not what you plan to do?" she whispered. Her eyes rested upon him for only an instant then flickered to the window of the coach, seeing the wide gates of the castle pass by.

"I had hoped to make this mutually pleasurable, Lisette. You are a very attractive woman."

"I don't want to be with you," she whispered, her voice hardly loud enough for him to hear. "I love another."

Rodbert stared at her for a moment, his body rocking with the movement of the carriage. Her pretty green eyes darted from his face to the window and then back, finally meeting his as if to challenge him. "I am no ogre to take a woman who does not want me," he said finally. "If you love another, how is it you didn't speak up at the wedding?"

"You'd have banished my father," she said, her voice showing her pique.

He tipped his head to the side, studying her. "We shall have the marriage annulled," he said slowly. "You shall stay with me at my castle only as long as is necessary to provide the legal documentation. Would that make you happy?"

"Yes, oh yes," she repeated, a smile gracing her sweet lips. "Would you really do this?"

"No, of course not," he grinned. "You're my wife and the soon to be mother of my child. How could you believe anything so stupid?" He reached out, grabbing her around the waist while she stared at him in confusion and dragging her onto his lap. His hand slid over the front of her gown, pinching the nipple he could feel through the thin fabric.

"No...stop," she cried, fighting his hands only to feel his palm strike her cheek. The blow was not hard enough to bruise, but it was enough to shock her into being still.

"I don't want to hurt you, Lisette, but I will if you refuse to behave."

Tears streamed down her eyes, her face stung from his blow. His hands now moved over her body, taking her stunned silence as her willingness to do as he wished. She felt the coach rumble over the final bridge, heard the loud echoing sound the wheels made as it went under the thick walls of the gate.

Her eyes were huge, luminescent with her tears. She stared up at him as he groped the small curve of her breasts, his other hand working its way up her skirts. "Please," she whispered.

"Please what, Lisette? Please make love to you? Please kiss you? Please *fuck* you?" he asked cruelly. "If you are asking please for anything else, you might want to rethink it. I shan't take it well if I must listen to your whining once more."

He spread her thighs, forcing her to face him, straddling his loins. The position pushed up her skirts, exposing her to his eyes and fingers. "How very pretty," he growled, his fingers playing with the red curls that matched the ones upon her head. "Such white skin against these pretty curls. Are you wet for me, Lisette?"

She cringed, trying to pull away from his hands. But instead, he grabbed her, holding her so that he could push his fingers into her dry flesh, poking and prodding cruelly. His palm rubbed cruelly at her mound, mashing the small bead of her clit with brutal intensity. "Stop!" she cried, her fists pushing against his chest even as she tried to rise from his lap. Before she realized what she was doing, her hand flashed out, leaving a nasty red mark across his handsome face. Silence fell over the carriage, leaving no sound but for the wheels turning and the springs squeaking. Even the sounds of the horses seemed loud as she stared at Rodbert in horror. His eyes blazed, his face grew hard. Reaching between them, he fumbled with ties, pulling free his massive organ, throbbing with his lusty pulse.

"I had thought to show you pleasure, to make this taking of your virginity one that you would find enjoyable." He shook his head, grasping her hips and drawing her closer to the tip of his swollen glands. "Now I see you'd rather have it rough and forego the gentleness I'd planned upon."

"No, please. Don't do this here!" she cried.

He felt the tip of his cock push into her vaginal opening, her dryness causing her pain and him some discomfort. He spit into his hand, rubbing the saliva over himself before trying again. Taking her hips in his hands once more, he drew her down, inching into her tightness until he was seated inside of her.

"You have no barrier," he growled, his hand coming up to jerk her face up to his. "Who did you give your innocence too?"

His eyes blazed, anger making his hands rough, his expression hard. "Tell me who?" he growled again when she didn't answer him.

The scream came from just outside the coach, startling Prince Rodbert enough that he released his grip upon Lisette, allowing her to scramble off of his lap, her cunny burning from his rough possession. She'd barely returned to her own seat, frantically pushing down her skirts when, with a loud crunch, the carriage jerked and seemed to jump, the horses screaming as their traces cut into their sides. Prince Rodbert grabbed for the edge of the window just as the carriage shook, falling on to its side with a loud shrieking crunch. Lisette felt her body soar for a split instant and then a terrible pain slammed into the side of her head and her vision dimmed. The sound of battle, of men screaming, of swords clanging together were the last thing she heard as darkness took her.

Chapter Six

The sound of chains roused her, calling Lisette from her blanketed cocoon of blackness and into the light. She blinked her eyes, trying to force them open, struggling against the dark that wanted to suck her back in. With a sigh, she finally was able to concentrate on one thing, almost shrieking when she saw what it was.

A black cross hung above her head, the top pointed downward. Next to it, a small chicken had been placed, its body twisted, its head missing. Blood stained the white feathers and even as she watched, one floated down to land against her body. A shiver of revulsion took her and she tried to get up, to get away from this hellish place.

Her arms were tied above her head, the ropes biting into her skin, another set were around her ankles tying her to the corners of the table she was placed upon. Lisette lifted her head, her eyes focusing on the candles that had been placed strategically around her body. One sat between her thighs, the flame close enough to the curls on her mound to let her feel the heat. Another was by each ankle and then more by her face. She was stretched so tightly, she couldn't move.

She turned her head, trying to see into the blackness that surrounded her, hearing voices and noises beyond the light of the candles. "Who's there?" she called, her voice quivering in fear and cold.

A black robed figure appeared, a cowl pulled over the person's face leaving him in shadow. He hesitated above her, his hands reaching out to stroke lightly over the skin of her arm, making her flinch in distaste.

"Please, let me go," she begged that strange figure, wishing she could see his eyes. "Please, my father is King Maxim; he will pay for my safe return."

The stranger's hand slipped lower, playing over her arm and shoulder and then resting with gentle duplicity upon the curve of her breast.

Lisette stared down in horror, only then realizing that she was naked, her body exposed to anyone's eyes. She cringed, wanting to cry out as he plucked at her pale nipple that was already hard in the cold air. Her heart picked up its beat as he twisted the pebbled tip, squeezing and rubbing it between his harsh fingers.

Another figure soon joined him, this one smaller, the cowl decorated with designs of ancient runes, depicted in silver and gold thread. Gems adorned the small hands that came out from the folds of the robes, lifting a small bottle and pouring the fluid inside onto her palms.

Starting with Lisette's shoulders, the robed woman slowly spread the scented oil across Lisette's bare skin, seeming to take delight in stroking and kneading her flesh until a moan of forced pleasure was torn from Lisette's lips. Her fingers were warm, the oil heated between their flesh, making her skin glimmer in the flickering light of the candle.

Soon the man's hands were covered in the oil also and he moved to her feet, rubbing the oil with gentleness into her heels, moving in slow circles up and over her ankles, around her calves and over her knees. Her thighs were caressed even as she fought to move away from the tender touch.

"No!" she cried, doing her best to pull away. "Don't touch me!"

"The cup," the first robed figure hissed, his voice distorted and unrecognizable. "She must be willing if this is to work."

The smaller figure picked up the cup, holding it reverently between her palms. She handed it to the man, speaking words in a language that Lisette could not understand.

"Hold her head," the man said, lifting the golden cup and raising it above his head.

Lisette cried out as small but strong hands gripped her head, holding her still no matter how hard she struggled. She watched as his hand moved closer, the cup tilting above her mouth. A tiny dribble of thick fluid spilled from the edge, falling to her lips even as she writhed to get away.

Her nose was pinched, leaving her with no choice but to breathe through her mouth, choking as the liquid, dark and bitter, fell upon her tongue. She swallowed convulsively, gagging at the foul taste.

It began working on her almost immediately, the potent brew swimming through her system, causing her breasts to swell with desire, her nipples to harden to tiny diamond-like points. An almost unquenchable desire boiled in the depths of her belly and she could feel her sex pout, growing wet with desire. A moan tore from her throat and she began to struggle, but this time for a completely different reason.

It was as if a fire had been set to blaze inside her most secret soul, consuming her until she could do nothing but plead for release from its heat. Her legs fought to close, to rub against anything that would give her some kind of relief.

"Oh!" she cried, her breathing growing heavy and short. Her eyes dilated with her arousal, the green disappearing until it was nothing but a tiny ring around her pupils. Her head tossed against the table she was tied to, her back arching with need. "Please," she growled. "Please make it stop!"

The man lifted his head, his grin shining whitely in the dark of the room. He lifted his hands to the cowl, slowly lowering it. "She is ready," he declared to the woman. "Remove your robe and prepare yourself."

Edwina unhooked the front of the very heavy robes, letting them fall from her naked shoulders with a soft sigh. Even at her age, she had a body that was beautiful and sleek, a body any woman would envy. Her breasts were high and firm, round with large brown nipples that contracted in the cold. A slender stomach, taut muscles and lush, full hips sat above long, curved legs. Her sex was bare of hair, the lips thick and swollen, her clit peeping out between. Edwina's thighs glistened with her excitement, made even more so by the gift she would receive from her stepdaughter.

The gift of youth and beauty, of energy and firm, toned skin, it was everything she could ever think of wanting. With this gift, she could go anywhere and never have to worry. Men were easily led, swayed by a pair of firm breasts and a tight cunny to cradle their lusty cocks. She went to the head of the table, leaning down to kiss Lisette's mouth.

"Darling stepdaughter, you don't know how much I appreciate your sacrifice. Trust that I will remember you with a fondness that I feel for no one else." She smiled, stroking over

Lisette's cheek. The girl's hands, tied as they were, brushed against the bare flesh of Edwina's mound, making her press herself tighter to the lust-filled young woman.

"Let us begin," Edwina said, her voice anxious and eager now that the moment was close to hand.

"Come closer, come closer," the man called to the darkness around Lisette. Men began to move closer to the table, unhooking their robes and letting them fall where they may. Each man was naked under the full robes, their cocks rising as they came closer to the beautiful, young princess.

A small wooden bowl was passed from one man to the other, each dipping their fingers into the sweetly fragrant contents. Finally, it was handed to Edwina. She touched the dips of her fingers into the oily substance, smiling at the scent. Her eyes sparkled as she looked at the only member of their group still dressed.

"Her breasts must be anointed, each nipple must be teased erect. Her sexual energy will consume her flesh, sending her into a frenzy of desire that none but the man of her dreams would be able to assuage. When it completely consumes her, then you shall drink of her nectar. If all goes as planned, you shall grow younger and be in better shape almost immediately. But if it doesn't," he paused, feeling the eyes of all upon him. "If one thing deviates from the potion, then you, your Majesty, will feel the bite of age."

"I understand," Edwina said, her body impatient to begin. She wanted only to feel the skin of this pale beauty against hers, to taste her flesh, to nuzzle at the juncture of her thighs and feed of the power of her sex. Nothing could compare to the feel of that energy, of that sexual surge of strength that she would feel when the moment of completion of the spell was done.

She felt her companion, Jasper, come up behind her, his hands resting lightly upon her slim, naked shoulders. He leaned forward, his breath heating her skin, his palms lightly caressing her slender arms. "Ready, Edwina?" he asked, feeling her stiffen at the familiarity he used.

"Yes," she said, the word barely more than an exhaled whisper.

"Place your hands upon her shoulders, your fingers pointing toward her breasts." He spoke slowly, his words distinct as he began the ancient chant. His body began to sway, the men around them swaying in time. Their voices rose as they joined in with the chant, the sound echoing in the chamber.

"Pick up the chalice," Jasper whispered, letting the crowding men continue with the chant as he directed Edwina in the proper sequences. He held out a long, sharp knife. "Slice the tip of your finger, let the blood drip into the chalice."

He watched as she did as he said, smiling when she didn't flinch at the pain of the knife. Her blood dripped into the chalice, mixing with the herbs and wine he'd mixed earlier. "Use the same finger and trace the form of the pentagram upon her body, the top most point must rest between her breasts for that is the source of her power."

Edwina flinched this time as the mixture covered the wound of her finger, the alcohol burning her skin. She made the pentagram, closing her eyes as she connected the magical symbol, praying to the god of her powers for his guidance and good will.

Jasper moved forward once more, taking the chalice from Edwina, lifting it to his lips to drink of the magical mix. It was potent, bitter and he gagged but once, swallowing all but the tiniest of dregs at the bottom. He turned, setting it down and closing his eyes as the brew filled his belly, the power of the potion spreading outward in a harsh heat that cramped his bowels.

His knees weakened, but he persevered, determined to gain as much of the power of Edwina as was possible for him to do. One of the chanting men moved forward, his eyes upon his Master. He placed his hand upon the groaning man's shoulder, wanting to help.

Jasper swung around, seeing the accolade in front of him, the concern in the man's eyes. Leaning forward, he whispered words into the man's ear, watching as he ran from the room to do Jasper's bidding.

"Now," he said his voice husky with pain. "You must arouse her with your touch, fill her with a longing to feel your kiss between her thighs. She must beg for you to end her torment, my queen. That is when you must drink from her." He moved around to the other side of the table, watching as Edwina began to weave her magical desire around Lisette.

Under his robes, his cock hardened with desire for the virginal beauty with her long sweep of red hair and her mystical green eyes. He could feel the queen's power as well, for now that he'd drank her blood along with the potion, her strengths were his.

"Yes," he hissed softly, his fingers trembling as if they were touching Lisette's soft skin. "Arouse her, my queen, drive her mad with passion."

* * * *

Lisette looked up, her eyelids barely parted, seeing Gifford standing above her head. His hands were upon her skin, caressing her, stroking her with the fire of his touch. His eyes were on her, roaming the softness of her curves, his lips parted as he drove her mad.

He touched her nipples, fingers rolling the taut buds, squeezing and rubbing them until she moaned her pleasure, squirming against the bindings that held her to the table. She wanted to touch him too, she wanted to pull him between her legs and feel the magic of his possession once more.

"Gifford!" she cried, her head falling back against the table. "I love you."

"No, my beauty," Gifford said, his voice sounding strange. "No, it is not Gifford that you want. It is Edwina."

The words barely penetrated Lisette's desire fogged conscience and she stared at him, not comprehending what he was saying. "No, I want you. I want you inside of me. Please," she groaned, wiggling her hips as much as she could.

His hands stroked over her stomach, teasing the slight dip of her navel, the softness of her lower belly right above the sweet curls of her mound. Her thighs were tensed as she held her breath, waiting for him to move lower, to touch her between the swollen wet lips of her needy sex. "Please," she sighed again.

Hands touched her thighs, smoothing the soft skin so close to her heat that she jerked against the ropes, the pain bringing her to herself for a single instant. That instant was long enough for her eyes to open wide, seeing Edwina over her, the Queen's hands upon her body, stroking her.

"No!" she cried, the sound echoing in the stone chamber. "Stop, leave me alone!"

"Give her more," Jasper said, coming to stand next to the table.

"Too much more will kill her," Edwina growled, lifting the small cup of thick brew.

"Not enough and she won't want you, then you will fail," Jasper snapped back at her. "Hold her nose."

Lisette struggled but she was no use for the strength of the evil queen. With a moan of defeat, her mouth opened to breathe and the potion dripped between her lips. She tried desperately to spit it away, but Edwina poured more into her mouth, then clamped it shut until Lisette was forced to swallow. Pain tore through her, radiating from her swollen sex and making her scream.

"No," Edwina whispered as she watched her stepdaughter writhe in pain.

"You must continue," Jasper growled, taking Edwina's hands in his own, and placing them upon Lisette's contorting body. "If you don't, she will die leaving your spell unfinished. You will be made to pay by the powers that be. Finish this, or suffer what consequences they decide to visit upon you."

* * * *

Gifford stared up at the stars flickering in the onyx black sky above him. The moon hung full and heavy, sitting just above the trees. He walked alone, a stick in his hand that he used to swipe at the bushes beside the road when the anger and agony of what he was feeling grew too big to contain.

The sight of Lisette, his beautiful Lisette, her hair up in curls standing before the castle priest with that royal, speaking those words, those very words that would take her away from him forever, it was one he would never forget. He couldn't, the pain, the misery of that sight would be with him forever.

"Damn her," he growled. "Damn her for making me love her." He swung the thick stick so hard that it busted in two against one of the branches of a tree, sending a shower of bark and leaves to fall around him. "Aaahhhh!" he shouted, throwing his head back and letting out the roar that clogged his chest.

Safford cringed at the sound, never having seen his brother in such pain. He hurried his step, knowing that the news he carried would be unwelcome, but also knowing that Gifford should be informed.

"Giff?" he called, clearing his voice and trying again. "Gifford!"

"What?" he roared, turning his head to stare at his brother. "Leave me alone, Saff. I…I don't want anyone around now."

"No, I can't, you have to know…"

"I don't want to know anymore. How could she? I thought… Fuck me, I guess I thought wrong." He hung his head, throwing away the small piece of the stick he still carried. "I just don't care anymore."

"She didn't want to marry him, Giff. She was coerced by the Prince and her father."

"What does it matter now? The deed is done. She is his wife and out of my reach." He growled deep in his throat as the pain rose within him again.

"No, wait Giff, let me finish, please," Saff almost begged, knowing the stubborn closed look on his brother's face boded ill for him. "Just hear me out."

Giff turned quickly, his hand fisted. That fist flashing toward Safford's face only to stop at the last possible second. "Why do you not hear me? I do not care anymore. She made her choice."

"She was not given a choice to make, not one she could with any kind of conscience. I have spoken to people, Giff. They said that King Maxim signed a deal in his grief over her disappearance with Prince Rodbert. He pledged to help find the Princess in return for her hand in marriage. The marriage was to be done in proxy if she hadn't been found." Saff ducked as Giff tried to hit him again. This time the punch went above his head and he stepped under it, grabbing his brother's arms.

"If she hadn't married him, King Maxim would have lost his kingdom to Prince Rodbert. Do you understand, Giff? She married the scoundrel to save her father."

"And I ask again, why does this have to do with me? She can't be with me. She married him. She said her 'I dos', I heard 'em loud and clear." He struggled to free himself but Saff wasn't budging.

Saff struggled with him, holding him with a grip of iron. If he got free there would be hell to pay and he would be the one paying it. "Listen you dunderhead, Lisette is missing! The carriage she was traveling in was found tipped over. Rodbert is dead!"

Giff stopped fighting, his breath hissing in his lungs. "What?"

"Rodbert was found in the carriage, his neck was broken and there was a dagger in his chest. Lisette was missing, though there was blood upon the seat and on the outside door handle. The traveling party was attacked, the horses spooked until they ran." Safford slowly released Giff, ready to duck in case he decided to try and knock him down again. "The king has men out searching for her. He says the dagger belongs to his wife, Queen Edwina."

"The queen took a whip to Lisette, Saff. I saw the marks on her back. That bitch is up to no good." He turned suddenly, seeing his brother flinch away from him. "We've got to go look for her. If the Queen has her..." he couldn't finish, the thought setting his blood to ice.

"Mall should be here with the horses," Saff said, his hand going to Giff's shoulder, squeezing reassuringly. "We'll find her, Giff, then you can give her this and she can come back where she belongs, with you." He handed his older brother the small emerald he'd pocketed the other day, now set in a gold setting. It seemed to catch the light of the stars, sparkling mysteriously up at him as he cradled the small token in the palm of his hand.

"When did you...?"

"When we got the other gems out. I thought it would make a fine bride's gift."

"It does," Giff said, his eyes going to Saff. "Thank you."

"Well hell, man. We can't have you messing up with the girl, it could wreck the Tunsey reputation." Saff slapped him on the back, hearing the sound of horse hooves. "There's Mall. Where do you suppose we should start looking?"

"The queen wouldn't be stupid enough to go to her own chambers with Lisette. She must know that she'd be suspect." Giff pocketed the small ring, the slight weight feeling heavy in his pocket as he thought of the woman he loved, wondering if he'd ever have the chance to give it to her. He shook the thought away, concentrating upon finding her. "She would need somewhere to keep her, somewhere no one would think to look..." His head snapped up and his eyes met Saff's.

"What?" the younger man asked, seeing the look in his brother's brown eyes.

"The cliffs, there are enough caves in those cliffs to hide in, they are close and no one would suspect she would go there." He watched as Mall galloped past, tossing each of the other two men reins to the horses that followed them. "But which one," he wondered.

He swung up on the horse, turning it quickly and then kicking his heels in. The horse reared before jumping forward to a gallop. Mall quickly followed, Saff right behind him, their horses kicking up a cloud of dust as they raced off.

* * * *

King Maxim stared at the body of Prince Rodbert, his eyes upon the blade that still pierced his breast. He'd recognized it instantly as belonging to his wife and Queen. Sadness consumed him even as worry had him up and pacing. If Edwina had taken Lisette... he couldn't think of the danger his daughter was in.

He stared up, his hand on his heart. "Watch out for her, my love. Keep our daughter safe."

"Your Highness!"

Maxim turned, hope in his gaze. "What is it? Have you found her?"

"No, there are men at the door. They say they know where Lisette could be!"

Maxim rushed forward, grabbing the man's arm. "Where are they? Send them in, send them in now."

84

Chapter Seven

Gifford galloped quickly down the rocky slope that led to the sandy white beaches that ran the length of the coastline, backing into mostly rocky cliffs. The night sky was alight with stars, the moon hanging low and full, beautiful above him. He was reckless as he kicked the horse into a more frenzied step, caring little of the beast or of his own mortality as he could think only of his Lisette.

She was at the hands of the queen, he knew it, he could almost feel her terror calling to him. They were somewhere up there, in one of the many caves that dotted the rocky face of the cliffs. He let his instincts take him, guiding the gamely running horse by feel.

He'd sent his brothers to the King, ordering them to bring men back, for he didn't know how big of a group had attacked Prince Rodbert's party. But he'd refused to wait. She was in danger and he couldn't stay still. He had to find her.

The horse's hooves sounded with a thundering beat as he galloped up the sandy shoreline. He studied each cave carefully, hoping to find some sign, a clue that Lisette was inside of one of them. If he had to stop and check each cave, he'd never find her in time.

"Come on, Lisette," he called softly, closing his eyes for just an instant. "Tell me where you are."

* * * *

Her heart was pounding, beating almost painfully hard in her chest; her eyes were wild as they swept around the strange looking room. Hands touched her sensitive skin, groping at her, fingers pulling apart the lips of her cunny, plunging inside. Her head tossed, her hair flinging into her face as she tried to make sense of what was happening to her.

Come on, Lisette Gifford's voice seemed to float to her. *Tell me where you are.*

"I'm here," she croaked, her voice harsh with the effects of whatever they'd given her. "Help me, Gifford!"

Warm lips found the tip of her breast, a tongue swirled around it, pulling and tugging, before biting delicately upon the

85

pale pearl. She moaned, hating that she felt such rampant desire, such need. Her hips moved restlessly, her back arching against the cold table, pressing her to those soft lips that much harder.

"She is ready," a deep voice said above her head and Lisette opened her eyes, watching as the man who still wore his robe moved between her thighs. "The little Princess is wet and hot. I think she likes your lips upon her breast, my Queen."

"Finish the ceremony," Edwina snarled, wanting it over so that she might leave these ignorant men and return to her life of ease. "I want her dead before anyone might find us."

Jasper lifted a knife above his head, the dagger was long, jeweled with a rippled blade. He moved it above Lisette, tracing the patterns of the ancient runes above her long body with the tip. "The ancients move among us, granting us our powers. With this sacrifice of virgin's blood, I give back to you my forever loyalty and promise. Take this sacrifice, feed from her, feel her energy and power. Grant us your favor."

He leaned forward, moving the candle that had been between her legs. "Kneel upon the table," he told Edwina. When she did as she was bade, Jasper filled the chalice with a mixture of ground herbs and sweet red wine, stirring the mixture with his own finger, leaking his own blood into the mix. If the queen had any idea about what he had planned, she would have him killed. Hopefully, by the time she had any inkling, it would be too late. Her powers would be his and she would be nothing but a dried husk, ready to blow away at a stiff wind. He almost rubbed his hands at the thought.

"Drink," he urged. "Empty the cup."

Edwina took a long pull of the liquid, almost gagging at the foul taste. "Do you poison me?" she asked her man as she held the cup away from her lips.

"No, tis but the herbs that make the mix so awful, my Queen. Drink, leave nothing in the cup if you wish this potion to work." Jasper forced himself to stare into Edwina's eyes. He couldn't let her know what he was doing. His eyes glanced down at Lisette's beautiful body, smiling as he saw the pentagram upon her chest.

He knew the five pointed star drawn in the way he'd advised the queen would protect the lovely Princess from black magic, saving her from Edwina's evil. Only by drawing the pentagram upside down with the two bottom-most points drawn upward would make this pentagram one used for the devil's work. It was said that the two points were actually the horns upon the devil's head, invoking his image.

But with white magic, Lisette would be able to withstand Edwina's evil and he would, with the exchanging of blood in the cups, draw Edwina's powers into himself. "Drink it all, my queen," he whispered, watching as she held the cup to her mouth, tilting it as she threw her head back, determined to finish the foul brew.

He felt a rumble deep inside his chest, a burning that should have hurt him terribly but he only felt a sensual caress of the flicker of flames. The dagger was raised and as soon as Edwina finished her cup, Jasper was ready to recite the other part of the potion, having already changed it to add the required lines to fool the queen.

"Hold the last in your mouth, do not swallow."

Edwina nodded, her cheeks puffed out as she did as he said. The awful taste made her want to gag. The smell was horrendous. It took all her will to hold the nasty liquid upon her tongue, waiting for Jasper's next command.

Jasper drew closer yet, his hand going to Lisette's cunny, drawing open the thick lips. "Let it drip from your mouth," he urged. "Let it fall upon the sex of the sacrificial."

A little at a time, Edwina did as she was bid. She listened to Jasper's deep voice speaking the lines of the potion, his tone one of utmost reverence. When Lisette's cunny was covered with the brew, Jasper pushed Edwina's head down, holding her against Lisette's body. "She must come, my Queen, if this spell is to work."

Edwina was no stranger to the flavor and scent of aroused female. Her tongue slipped out between her parted lips, taking a taste of her stepdaughter. The potion dribbled over her sex was bitter, but under it was a hint of Lisette's sweetness. She ran her tongue over the pink, wet flesh, moving with practiced sensual rhythm. Lisette moaned, her eyes closing as the Queen's talented tongue wriggled over her clit before thrusting inside of her.

Behind the queen, Jasper pressed close, his robe opening to expose a rock hard cock. He rubbed the swollen shaft against Edwina's softness, feeling her dripping wet and hearing her gasp. She lifted her head, her lips shiny with Lisette's sweetness. "This is not part of the spell," she gasped.

"No, my Queen. But the more sexual energy filling the room, the more your spell will work. I wish to bind myself to you, give to you pleasure and see to your needs," he said, his eyes downcast so that she could not see into his thoughts.

Edwina did not look convinced but Lisette was warm and moaning beneath her and her own body was turning traitor, craving the feel of Jasper's hard cock deep inside her own sopping cunny. Desire pooled in her own loins, making her feel hot and needy, desperate to be fulfilled. She moaned softly before making her decision.

"Do it," she whispered, turning back to the treat before her.

Jasper rammed himself home in one quick, hard thrust, feeling Edwina's cunny clutch around his cock. Wet heat surrounded his staff, gripping him tightly, seeming almost to suck him inside the witch queen's body. Her gasp of surprise met his of pleasure, mingling in the damp, still air of the room. Around them, the acolytes continued their chanting, each man slowly stroking himself to climax.

* * * *

Gifford spotted the light shining dimly from the cave entrance, his eyes narrowing as he stared. If he hadn't been looking for that small glimmer, he wouldn't have seen it, so soft a light to be almost indistinguishable. The cave was up the beach, well above the tide line. He kicked his horse, speeding toward it.

"Hang on, Lisette. I'm coming," he growled.

To reach the cave, he had to maneuver up a small path, actually little more than a rocky trail that wound its way up the front of the cliff. He left his horse on the beach, the path being too narrow for the beast to walk. Hopefully, Mall and Saff would find the animal and figure out where he'd gone.

As he drew closer, he could hear the sound of chanting, guttural and deep, evil sounding. He came upon a small ledge and carefully peered inside the cave.

The light shone through a small room, showing another crack in the cave wall where the chanting and the light came from. He hurried through the first part of the cave, slipping silently through the crack and down a narrow hall. At the end of that natural hallway was another entrance and he slipped silently through that as well.

Surrounded by candles, he could make out Lisette's soft naked form lying on top of a wooden table. A woman knelt between her legs, a man behind her, his cock thrusting urgently inside of the kneeling woman. Around them, ten men stood naked, their hands vigorously stroking their cocks, watching as Lisette was forced to submit to the queen.

He had no weapon but for the knife he kept at his side and his own size and strength. Hearing Lisette cry out, her voice almost wailing with agonized pleasure, he rushed forward, grabbing the first two men before they knew he was there and bashing their heads together.

He let them fall, spinning to face the next man, laying him out easily with a blow from his huge fist to the man's chin. The fourth came in low, trying to ram him in the belly. Giff sidestepped him, watching as his lunge took him off balance and he hit the rocky wall.

The acolytes, now only numbering six, turned upon him en masse and Gifford grunted, feeling his arms drawn behind his back, his body being forced to the floor. With a growl of rage, he shifted under the weight of the men, feeling feet kicking furiously at his sides. He forced himself to his feet, shaking off the man who held his arms, his elbow connecting solidly to the man's nose, blood spurting upon the floor.

They surrounded him, five naked men, keeping him from his Lisette. He could hear her moans, the sexual pleasure she was receiving making her sound almost animalistic. His eyes darted to her for a moment, seeing the confused expression upon her face.

Edwina and the man thrusting into her from behind continued their play as if he'd never interrupted. Jasper's hard hands were on her hips, pulling her rounded butt into him with every brutal thrust. His head was thrown back, his eyes closed tightly as if he savored every minute inside Edwina.

When Gifford reached them, he planned to kill the man with his bare hands and bring the queen back to her husband for his discipline. But for now, he had five men to dispose of.

With a roar of rage, the five charged him at once, Giff going down in a tangle of arms and legs.

* * * *

Safford bowed before the king, hitting Mall in the thigh with a well-aimed punch when he just stood gawking at the riches around him. "Your Highness, we come with news of your daughter."

"Where is she?" Maxim yelled, grabbing Safford's arm. "Tell me man, where is my daughter?"

"We believe she is in one of the caves by the beach, Sire." Saff watched as the man's eyes narrowed and then grew hopeful. "My brother is on his way there now."

"Who are you men? How do you know of my daughter?" Maxim growled, unease forming a ball in his belly.

"The princess found her way to our cabin when she ran away, Sire. She was with us for the few days she'd disappeared. My brother, Gifford, and her, well they fell in love." Mall stepped forward as he spoke, neither bowing nor kowtowing to King Maxim. "He wants to marry her."

"Mallory!" Saff growled, appalled at the way his younger brother was talking to the king. "Mind your manners, brother, or else you might find yourself up for another whipping."

Mall snorted, rolling his eyes. "You haven't been able to beat me nor whip me in years, Saff, don't think you can start now."

"My Lisette is in love?" Maxim asked slowly as if trying to get a hold of the thought. "Why did she not tell me?"

"Did you give her time to?" Mall asked. "Or did you just rush her off to be married the moment she returned home?"

"I had no choice. Prince Rodbert was holding my kingdom hostage with his scroll. If I didn't do as he said..." Maxim dropped his head unable to look either man in the eyes as the shame of what he'd done rolled over him. "I have no excuse," he said finally.

"Rodbert is dead. Lisette is not. You have time to make it up to her, but we must have men to go and save her. Knowing my brother, he's already there."

Maxim grabbed a satin swaged bell pull that was hanging in the corner of the room, giving it a hearty yank. Servants came running and then were sent scurrying as Maxim shouted orders. Safford and Mall didn't wait for the king's men to make ready, instead, rushing to their horses and starting off before them.

Safford knew Giff would go into the cave with no one to back him up. He would fight whomever he had to; do anything, to get Lisette back.

"We have to hurry," Mall said, echoing Saff's thoughts.

* * * *

Lisette couldn't breath. Flames of passion were burning at her soul and a strange pulling sensation began in the pit of her belly. It seemed to grow as the tongue that was even now torturing her cunny grew more frenzied in its attack. "God!" she cried, barely able to stand the pleasure that was turning slowly to pain. "Gifford!"

Giff heard his name, ducking a punch that would have smashed into his already bruised face. His body ached, his head hurt but none of that mattered. All that mattered was that he reach Lisette before whatever spell the queen was trying to do to hurt her.

His fist knocked down another of the acolytes and then another, breaking a hole through their human barrier that tried to keep him from Lisette. He plowed through it, his hand out to pull the queen from Lisette. Before he could, she gave a little cry, a whimper that sounded as a mixture of pain and pleasure and stiffened under the man who still thrust inside her body.

"What...?" Edwina cried, her eyes going to her hands as pain became focalized in her body. Her nails looked brittle, her fingers drying up. They curled at the edges, growing old and scarred looking, loosing any factor of youth and beauty. "What is going on?" she screamed, trying to push away from Jasper and only succeeding in breaking off the tips of her fingers.

Jasper felt the power rush through is body, his head spinning with the intensity of it. She tried to push him away, to fight him off but he would not be denied. Her powers were a heady mixture, her energy sweet and succulent. He would not quit until he had them all.

His hands kept hold of her hips, his cock thrusting furiously into the sweet sheath of her vagina. He felt her hands crumble against his arms, heard her shrieks of pain and torment.

Lisette looked up as Gifford appeared over her. She could hear Edwina's screams echoing through out the chamber. Tears fell from her eyes in a torrent of misery and need.

"It's all right, Lisette," he said, using his dagger to cut the ropes binding her hands to the table. One of the acolytes tried to stop him and he ducked down, pulling Lisette out of the way as the man went flying over the table.

Then his dagger slid easily through the other rope, freeing her legs. He lifted her carefully in his arms, holding her high against his chest and pulling her away from the horror of what was happening upon the table.

Edwina's elbows were little more than dried out shells of skin, her shoulders withering in front of their eyes. Whatever was happening to the queen had begun on her toes as well, for her feet and ankles were crumbling, her legs looking like the skin that was peeled off when a snake grew.

"STOP!" Edwina screamed as Jasper slammed into her one last time, filling her with hot seed that seemed to only hasten the decay of her body.

The acolytes who'd been about to attack Gifford turned from the sight, running through the cave and out into the night. Jasper stood over what was left of the queen, watching as his semen leaked out of her now leather like skin. Her throat was dried, no sounds able to come out of her lips that crumbled at the edges.

Gifford held Lisette's face against his shoulder, not wanting her to witness such horror. He turned from the sight, his eyes meeting Jasper's once before he strode quickly from the cave's chamber, eager to be away from the madness occurring within.

Tiny whimpers of shock tore from Lisette's mouth, her body shivering in Giff's arms. She wrapped her arms around his neck, her face buried in the warm skin of his throat, trusting him to get her away from the insanity behind them.

"It's all right," he crooned as he hurried from the cave. "You're safe, Lisette."

The night air brushed over them, cool and crisp, a balm after the stuffiness of the caves and the smoke of the torches. Giff put

Lisette on her feet for a single moment, tearing off the thick leather jacket he wore and wrapping it around her. Then he picked her up once more, holding her close as he whistled for his horse.

Somehow he managed to get both of them on the saddle, Lisette seated crosswise with her legs over his thigh, his jacket tucked securely around her. She hadn't spoken since he'd rescued her, holding on to him with a grip that was almost painful. He tried to soothe her now, bending his head even as he turned the horse, kicking the animal into a gallop before anyone could come after them. He wasn't going to lose her again, he couldn't. It would kill him.

"I've got you, Lisette. I've got you little love. No one will hurt you again." He murmured the words, his mouth at her ear, hearing a strange sound come from her, half groan half growl, startling him.

The horse shied as they reached the end of the beach and he turned the animal, controlling him with his legs as well as the reins. Forcing the animal back into a gallop, he headed towards the woods, his ears attuned to any sound of being followed.

Gifford held Lisette to him tightly, shielding her from tree branches as he moved further into the dense forest. He could feel her shaking, her hands holding onto him, gripping his shirt with desperate fingers. He rode far enough into the forest to hide them from any pursuit, finally slipping off the horse and pulling her down in a small clearing.

A tiny stream burbled its meandering way through the grassy clearing, the sound of the water running over the stones was soothing and melodic to his ears. He brought Lisette closer to the stream, sinking down on his haunches and clutching her against him.

Staring down into her face, he was surprised by the fierceness he saw there, and the heat in her eyes as she stared at him. For an instant, he forgot what he was going to do, but then his jacket fell open and he saw the blood upon her chest. He reached into his pocket, pulling out the linen handkerchief that had been included in the clothing he'd bought, drawing it out and wetting it in the water of the stream.

"I'm going to lay you down here, Lisette. I just want to get this blood cleaned up," he said softly, his hand stroking over her cheek.

She didn't answer him, only stared at him with that same expression upon her face. She had to be in shock, Giff thought, brushing a stray lock of hair off of her face. Then he pulled open the jacket a bit farther, exposing the bruises and bumps she'd retained during the accident as well as the smear of blood and something else that coated the fine hair of her mound.

"Oh God," he whispered. "What did they do to you?" His hand shook as he slowly slid the wet cloth over her skin, scrubbing carefully at the dried stain on her stomach. He turned to rinse it in the stream, returning to his cleaning, glancing up every few moments to make sure he wasn't scaring her or hurting her.

His hand brushed against her softly rounded breast, and he was startled to hear Lisette moan. He snatched his hand away, afraid he had frightened or hurt her in some way. He was even more startled when she reached up, pulling his hand back to her breast, her fingers twining with his, over his, to draw him even closer.

"Please," she whispered, the need in her voice so evident, it was like a separate entity. "I...I hurt."

A rush of heated blood shot to his groin, his cock hardening against the pants he wore. He could feel her hand over his, the hard tip of her breast pushing against his palm as she pushed his fingers against her. Her body arched, her eyes closing upon a gasping moan as she tried to get closer. The way she looked, outlined by the lush grass of the clearing, her body naked but for his jacket that had mostly fallen away from her, he couldn't help the growl of lust that escaped him.

But his mind quickly intervened. He couldn't do this to her, she'd been hurt and abused. "Lisette," he whispered huskily, pulling his hand away despite her groan of disappointment. "I can't do this. *We* can't do this."

He watched as her hand slid over the flesh he just released, her body arching as her fingers plucked and pulled upon her rosy nipple, her head tossing against the grass. She moaned, crying out in pleasure, her eyes closing.

"Oh God!" he moaned, sounding like a man subjected to more pain than he could possibly handle. "Lisette, what are you doing?"

Her eyes flew open, those soft, lambent green eyes flying to his face. "I hurt," she whispered. "Touch me, please."

Her hand reached out, her fingers stroking over the corded muscles in his thighs, sliding up over the heavy bulge in the front of his pants. He jerked when she wrapped her palm over his erection, moaning as she moved, squeezing and rubbing his hard flesh. "God, Lisette, what did they do to you?"

Her cry and the obvious need to her voice had his body jerking under her hand. "T...they gave me something. P...Please help me."

Gifford slid his hand carefully down the front of her body, his eyes watching her face as he stroked through the sticky wetness that covered her mound. She parted her legs eagerly, groaning softly as his thick finger slid inside the sleek flesh of her sex, finding her sopping wet, her sheath clasping eagerly on his finger. Her hips moved, her breath coming in heated pants, whimpers of pleasure and desperate need escaping from her lips.

"More," she groaned, reaching up further, her fingers finding the buttons of his pants. "I...I need you in me."

He was at the edge of his control, his body shaking violently, wanting her with a desperation he could little resistance. It seemed as if he hadn't been inside of her in ages, instead of just days. When her fingers wrapped around his cock, pulling the long, hard length of it from his pants, he almost embarrassed himself right there. "Lisette," he growled, pulling away, his forehead resting against the skin of her shoulder. "It's too much, I want you too badly."

Her fingers gripped his arms, her nails digging into the taut skin. "Please," she begged helplessly. Her eyes were desperate; her lips seeking his as she wordlessly begged him, pulling at him to get him between her thighs.

Giff groaned, feeling the heat of her cunny, the stickiness of her mound against his hard flesh. She squirmed under him, her legs slipping up his, opening her to his penetration. He hesitated, not wanting to hurt her, not after everything she'd been through, but she slid her hands down his back, ending with her palms cupping his ass, pulling him against her.

"Love," he groaned, giving into her pleas, his cock finding and sliding deep inside of her in one smooth movement. She was like wet satin against him, tight and hot, drawing him deeper until he thought he would lose himself to her.

He rose on his elbows, holding his weight from her, his eyes roaming over her face, tracing the line of her throat, the curved dips of her collarbone, the slight swells of her breasts. Her nipples pebbled and tilted upward as if begging for his mouth to suckle and twist. He heeded that invitation, taking the sweetness of her into his mouth, drawing upon the taut tip until she cried out beneath him.

His passion was such that he went half crazed, stroking into her in hard, agonizingly sweet thrusts, hearing her cries of pleasure as urgings for him to continue, feeling her legs wrap around his hips, pulling him harder against her.

Gifford felt the first tingle of his body, that amazingly sensual sensation heralding his climax. He fought it, throwing his head back, his eyes half closed as he concentrated on holding back, wanting to hear Lisette's cries of fulfillment, knowing she'd found the same pleasure. To that end, he changed the angle of his strokes, his fingers slipping between them to find the pearled hardness of her clit, his thumb brushing over it, pinching it gently between his fingers.

It sent her over, her body convulsing and arching under his, her nails digging into the flesh of his back, her toes curling as ecstatic swirls of heat and tingling pleasure flooded her. Lisette cried out his name, her tone that of someone almost lost in the miasma of her climax, holding onto him for dear life.

With a growl of relief, he let loose the control he held, slamming into her. His orgasm pulsed out of him as his seed filled her depths with heat. It seemed to last forever, a climax more intense than anything he'd felt in his life.

When it was done, he collapsed upon her, barely holding up his weight on his elbows. His lips, soft and parted, found hers, kissing her with a gentleness he scarce knew he could feel. She lay beneath him, spent, her legs slipping off of him, her arms stroking his back slowly. "Lisette?" he breathed against her lips.

"Hmm," she moaned, unwilling to move enough to speak.

"Are you all right?" he asked, hating that he sounded like a small lad, needing reassurance.

"Yes," she sighed, her fingers sliding into his hair. "I missed you."

He pulled away, her words reminding him of their time apart. Rolling onto his back, he stared up into the night sky, trying to understand what he was feeling.

* * * *

Lisette felt him pull away from her and her heart fell. She turned her head, looking for him. "Gifford?"

He reached out and took her hand, drawing it to his lips. We should get you back to your father," he said finally.

"I don't want to go back there," she said, a hint of panic in her voice. "He will make me go back to Prince Rodbert. I...I can't do that."

"Your husband is dead," he said, the word sounding like a derisive insult.

She rolled to her side, her hand coming out to rest against his chest. "I thought as much," she whispered.

"If you knew, why did you say you didn't want to go back to the castle?"

"I was not sure. I...hit my head when the carriage rolled. I woke up back...back there." She lifted her head to look at him. "Can't I go with you?"

"Why?"

Her mouth opened but no sound emerged. She stared at him, her heart in her eyes, her emotions bared but unable to say what she felt in her heart.

"Is it that hard to say?" he asked her softly, his hand coming up to rest against her cheek.

Lisette closed her eyes, savoring the warmth of him, the familiar calloused palm, his scent. "I..." She took a deep breath, opening her eyes, a new determination flooding her. "I love you," she said, her voice strong.

Gifford's lips twitched and as she watched, a smile bloomed on his handsome, rugged face. It was almost angelic, that smile, making her feel as if the sun had just come out. "See, that wasn't so hard."

97

"Yes, it was."

He laughed, rolling to his side to lean over her, kissing her with a thoroughness that had her body clinging to his, her lips parting on a lust filled sigh. Her fingers threaded through his hair, tugging on the silky locks to bring him even further down on top of her.

"Insatiable," he whispered. "You're a minx, my love."

"Your love?" she asked quietly, her eyes searching his.

"You had a doubt. I don't get into fights with naked men every night, Lisette."

She couldn't help the laugh that trickled out at the image his words evoked. "I should certainly hope not."

He lifted his head, his hand clasping lightly across her lips, stopping her words. "Shh," he urged, coming to his knees beside her and buttoning up his pants. He kept a sharp eye on the trail he'd made coming into this glade even as he held out his hand, urging her to her feet and wrapping his coat securely around her.

"What is it?" she whispered.

"Riders. A lot of them. It could be my brothers with your father's men," he said, trying to calm the shudder of fear that shivered through her.

"Or it could be Edwina."

"I doubt that," he whispered shaking his head. "From what I saw, I don't think we shall have to worry about her again."

"I...I thought I dreamed that."

He shook his head and put a finger to his lips. Lisette stared off the way he was looking, hearing the sounds of hoof beats and feeling the ground shake with them. They were close by. She could feel the cold air on her legs, making her realize how exposed she was. Her hair fell about her shoulders, sticks and grass entwined in the once silky locks.

Gifford reached out absently as he stared off into the woods, drawing her into his arms, his hands running up and down her arms, warming her. She sighed, enjoying his caress and the caring he showed in the tender embrace.

"It is my brothers," he grinned, glancing down at her. "Come, we shall get you safely in the midst of your father's men and get you back to the castle."

"But…" she didn't finish her sentence, glancing down at her hands as he stared at her.

"But what?" he asked, standing and lifting her to her feet.

Lisette sighed when he steadied her still weak knees with his arm around her, holding her to him. "I wanted to go home," she said finally.

"Home?"

Lisette's eyes met his, her hand coming up to caress his cheek. "With you," she said softly.

* * * *

Safford pulled back on the reins so suddenly, his horse reared.

"What the fuck…. What are you doing, Saff?" Mall called, his horse swerving to miss Saff's.

"Didn't you hear that?"

Mall listened carefully, finally hearing what Saff had. "It's Giff," he grinned.

They turned their horses in time to see Giff ride out of the forest, Lisette cradled in his arms.

"You found her," Mall exclaimed.

"Yep, and a bunch of strange guys running around naked under some really smelly robes. There might be a few of them left around, if you guys are still in the mood for a fight." He grinned, as Saff and Mall seemed to pout for a second at being left out of the battle.

"What about the evil bitch queen?"

"I don't think she'll be giving anyone trouble anymore." Giff looked up as the king's men gathered round, staring at Lisette's exposed legs. "Give me your coat," he barked at Mall, taking the proffered jacket and draping it over Lisette's legs, tucking it in securely. "Why don't you boys go see if you can round up any of those naked robed men and bring them back in? I know I left a few of them unconscious."

"We are to escort Princess Lisette home," one of the armed guards spoke up, eyeing the three brothers and the half naked princess with a suspicion.

"We'll escort the Princess home," Saff spoke up. "Didn't you hear my brother? Now get and do what he said." He sighed in disgust when the men grumbled but then did as they were ordered. "They sure don't make guards like they used to," he said to Mall.

Mall just grinned. "You okay, Lisette?" he asked the woman bundled in his brother's arms.

"Yes," she nodded. "Now I am."

"Then let's get you to your Pa. I have a feeling there's going to be some more arguing yet tonight."

* * * *

"No! I forbid it." The King's roar filled the great room of the castle, echoing in the almost empty chamber. "You will be going nowhere but to your room."

"Father," Lisette said softly, staring up into the red face of her father. "I love Gifford and he loves me. I want to go with him."

"You are too young to know what you want," King Maxim argued, refusing to back down. "You don't have the experience to know your own mind."

"And you do?" Gifford growled, his arm going around the woman he loved. "Look what you've put her through by marrying that witch queen of yours."

"This is none of your business," Maxim growled right back, his face going even redder with embarrassment. "This is between my daughter and myself."

"It is my business…sire," Gifford added grudgingly. "Lisette will be my wife and the mother of my children. We'd rather have your blessings, but even without, she is going with me." He cleared his throat, glancing at Lisette for just a moment before he spoke again. "She could be carrying my child now," he blurted.

"*What!*" King Maxim exclaimed, rising from his throne and taking a threatening step forward. "You've debauched my daughter?"

"No!" Gifford shouted. "I made love to the woman I love. The very same woman that I intend to marry."

"Lisette?" Maxim growled. "What do you have to say about this?"

"Father," she began in a small voice, playing with the tie of the dress she now wore. She'd gone to her chamber to find that it had been cleaned and the remaining garments hung in her wardrobe. Grabbing the first dress that came to her fingers, she slid it on and hurried back down the steps wanting to be there when Gifford confronted her father. She sighed; it definitely wasn't going the way she'd hoped. "I'd like to explain if you'd calm down. Both of you," she finished, looking at Gifford.

He grumbled something but shut his mouth when she gave him a second look, standing next to her with his arm around her.

"Very well," Maxim snarled. "Explain, but it'd best be good."

"It is a lengthy story, father. It begins with me hiding here in this room and hearing Edwina's plans to kill me."

"What? Why didn't you come to me? I would have protected you."

"You couldn't see any of it. Edwina had blinded you to my situation, Father."

"How you missed the whipping that bitch gave her is beyond me?" Giff growled, his eyes rising to confront Maxim's.

"Whipping?"

"Her back is crisscrossed with scars."

"Gifford," Lisette growled, drawing his attention. "Hush, you aren't helping here." Giff shut his mouth, but he looked decidedly unhappy about it.

"It matters not now, Father. But she did plan to kill me. I had no choice but to run away. I slipped out the side gate in mama's garden and then ran to the woods. I traveled all night until I couldn't see any longer then I fell asleep. The next morning, I found a cottage in the woods. It belongs to Giff and his brothers. They let me stay with them where I would be safe." She turned to look up at Giff. "I fell in love with Gifford almost at first sight, father."

Giff took her hand in his, raising it to his lips. His eyes met hers and he found himself lost in the green depths until Maxim's loud clearing of his throat interrupted them.

Maxim stared between the two, feeling a sadness invade his soul. His last precious piece of his wife was leaving him. But after everything they had been through, he couldn't put himself in the way of their happiness.

"You will be living with him?" he asked quietly.

"Yes, father, but it is not far and I shall visit you." Lisette felt a soaring hope as she stared at Maxim, her hand clasping Gifford's.

"You saved my daughter not once, sir, but many times; times when it should have been me doing the saving and not you. Seeing that she loves you and that you love her, I cannot stand in the way of her happiness."

"Thank you, sire," Giff said, stepping forward to bow before Maxim as he hadn't before.

"You will keep her safe," he ordered, though his tone was friendlier, "and let her visit often?"

"As often as she wishes," Giff answered, feeling Lisette's hand once more entwine with his. "We hope you will come and visit also, sire."

Maxim nodded. Sadness consumed him but he refused to let them see. "You shall be married before you leave. Your brothers shall stay a few days to give you time for a honeymoon alone," he ordered, glancing behind Giff to see Saff send a broad smile his way. "Now, wake the priest, we shall have a wedding ere dawn breaks."

This wedding was different than the one before, Lisette unable to look away from Giff's handsome and dearly loved features. Her responses were given with a joyful tone and his were eager, said in his deep voice that sent a shiver of longing through her body. Her smile was wide, her beauty even more astounding in the eyes of the man who loved her with his entire being.

"I, Gifford Tunsey, take thee, Lisette Joan, to be my wedded bride," he said, his eyes for no one but her. Even as he promised to love in sickness and in health, for better or worse, he didn't look elsewhere, for she deserved to know that his promises were for her and her alone.

When the priest, still slightly testy after being woken from a sound sleep, pronounced them man and wife, Gifford wrapped his arms around her tiny waist, lifting her from the ground to meet the hunger of his kiss. It was only Saff's elbow jammed into his ribs that brought the happy groom back to where he actually was. He grinned down at his wife, noting her well kissed lips and her starry eyes and couldn't wait to get her alone.

King Maxim rose, banishing his sad thoughts in the face of his daughter's happiness. "I wish to give you a title," he said to

Giff, surprised when the man refused. "But you are married to a princess. How can you not be titled?"

"I am married to Lisette, a woman, not a title. I don't need any title to make me good enough for your daughter. All I need is her love." He turned and glanced down at his bride who smiled back up at him. "If we could get a bath brought up to our room, sire, we will retire for the night. We have to leave early in the morning."

Maxim stared after the man, shaking his head in amazement. Then he smiled, for it is what he would have said when he first married his own precious bride. He lifted his hand, waiting for the servant to come and then ordered the bath as well as a tray of food and wine to be delivered to Lisette's chambers.

* * * *

Gifford took his bride into his arms, holding her close as the door closed behind the last of the servants bringing in what had been ordered. "I think your father has given us his blessing," he said softly, bending his head to kiss her.

She melted into his arms, sighing softly as her lips clung to his. Giff smiled, knowing she could feel his lips turning up.

"Why are you smiling?" she breathed.

"Because I'm happy. You make me happy," he said, framing her face with his hands. "I've never felt so complete as I do now with you in my arms." His lips closed once more upon hers. But he kept it short, backing away when she tried to deepen the kiss. "Come, wife," he said grinning. "Let's take a bath."

"Together?" she asked, her eyes going to the tub.

Giff followed her eyes, seeing the steam rise from the water that rose close to the edge of the tub. "It's big enough," he mused before turning back to her. His nimble fingers turned her and then started working on the small buttons of her gown, pulling it free, stroking his hand gently over the soft flesh he exposed. Bending, he kissed the nape of her of her neck, his teeth racking tenderly over her skin, laving the small bite mark with his tongue.

"Mmm," she moaned. "A bath does sound really tempting right now."

"Yes, it does," he murmured in her ear, his breath heating her skin.

Her gown dropped to the floor, his hands making quick work of the soft linen shift she wore under it, leaving her naked to his eyes. Sliding his hands around her waist, he cupped her firm breasts in his huge hands, squeezing gently, rubbing with erotic intent.

She arched against him, her head pressing against his shoulder.

"I think I like you like this," he whispered. "Perhaps I should keep you naked all the time."

"It might be dangerous cooking like this," she said, making him laugh.

"Well, perhaps an apron then, just enough material to cover up the important bits." He nuzzled her neck, breathing in her scent. "Come on, before you catch a chill."

Moving behind her, he pushed her towards the tub, holding her hand to help her slip into the heated water. When she was seated, he stepped back, pulling off his jacket. Dropping it carelessly to the floor, he slipped out of his shirt and then his boots, kicking them eagerly off his feet. A button on his breeches popped off as he hastily pulled them open, pushing them down and off his legs quickly until he was naked. Then he stepped into the water behind her, not even noticing as the water sloshed over the edge.

His legs filled the bottom of the tub and he bent them, letting Lisette sit between, her sweetly curved bottom pressing against his hard cock. Her head fit in the crook of his neck, her eyes closed as she moaned her pleasure at being with him once more.

He moved her hair to the side, tipping her chin up and finding her lips, growling as she moved over him, his hand coming around her to cup her breast. Her nipples were hard, tickling his palm as he teased her with soft strokes.

The water flowed around them, spilling over onto the floor, though neither noticed, both lost in the wonder of each other, of being together and married. His hands were gentle upon her skin, careful upon the bruises that she'd gotten that day. He kissed each one, lifting her in his arms until she straddled his lap, his arm wrapping around her waist to keep her close.

"I came so close to losing you," he whispered, nibbling at her lips and then her jaw.

"But you didn't," she sighed, tipping her head to give him easier access to her throat. "And you won't."

"I know I won't. I couldn't live without you, Lisette," he said, suddenly serious, his warm brown eyes filled with love as he looked down at her. "I thought the pain of losing you would kill me."

"I never wanted to go," she whispered.

Gifford kissed her, the kiss quickly turning heated. "Maybe I should just wrap you up in cotton and keep you in my pocket," he joked.

"Then you'll take me out when you want to do this?" she asked, reaching between them and guiding his hard cock into her.

"Oh yes," he growled, his head falling back as her heat and wetness surrounded him. She was hotter than the water, somehow slicker, gripping him tightly as she began to move over him. "Slowly love. We have all night."

Her nipples brushed against his chest and he heard her gasp, felt her grip his cock with clenching muscles and gritted his teeth. "Keep that up and this will be over before we start," he growled.

He watched as she bit her lower lip, her hands coming up to rest against his shoulders. She rode him as he watched her, her strokes long and even and then short and fast. He could feel her nails digging into his shoulder, his eyes on her face as she tensed, clasping him tightly inside as her body exploded with ecstasy.

"Ah," Gifford moaned, holding her against him as she fluttered and convulsed against him. He fought his own pleasure wanting to see her come again, waiting until her eyes shut and her body relaxed against his chest. "Lisette," he whispered.

She forced open her eyes, looking up at him. "Yes."

"You might want to hang on to something."

"Why?" she whispered sleepily.

He grabbed her hips, his body slamming up into hers, startling her at first. But by the fourth thrust, she was moaning once more, a pained look of pleasure upon her beautiful features. His head was thrown back, his teeth gritted as he pushed inside of her.

Gifford felt her come once more, heard her cries of ecstasy and let himself go, his body fracturing into tiny pieces as he pulsed inside of her. A roar of pleasure erupted from him and he held her close, his cock spewing his potent seed inside of her.

When it was over, when he finally caught his breath, he lifted her from the tub, not bothering with the towels that had been left to warm in front of the fire, taking her to the bed instead. Laying her down on the soft sheets, he followed her, lying beside her. His hand stroked idly over her belly, his eyes following the sleek lines of her body, finally resting upon her stomach.

"I want a child," he said suddenly.

Lisette smiled, letting her hand slide over his. "I do, too."

Gifford grinned. His mouth lowered to hers, whispering against her lips. "Then maybe we should keep trying. You know these things don't always take the first time."

Lisette giggled, the sound sweet in the quiet of their room. "And sometimes not even after the fourth, or the fifth or…mmffph."

His lips stopped her words.

The End

Excerpt from Wendy Stone's next Tunsley book…Victoria

In the forest, just outside the village gates, a young lad sat upon a tree limb, his bow in his hands, an arrow notched and pulled, ready to fly. He kept his eyes on the prey he'd chosen, a fine looking buck with a rack to be proud of. Waiting for the perfect shot, he controlled his breathing and was just about to let the arrow fly when the buck jumped, a feathered projectile protruding from his side.

"Well, fuck me," the boy growled, his voice sounding very young and somewhat girlish. "Who's poaching on my deer?"

Letting the string relax, keeping the arrow notched, he easily dropped from the tree limb, his eyes on the surrounding area.

"Nice shot, Mall," Safford said, slapping his brother on the shoulder. "Lisette will enjoy the taste of a venison roast."

"He should feed us well for quite some time," Mall grinned, agreeing with his brother. It had been a good shot. He kept walking toward where the buck now laid, his side heaving in pain from the wound.

"What the…" he growled, when a young boy came out of the tree almost on top of him. The boy was short, with dark curly hair and big blue eyes surrounded by feminine looking lashes. There was enough dirt on the lad to replant a field and his hair looked as if someone had taken a knife to it and just chopped off bits and pieces to keep it out of his eyes.

"Get out of the way, boy. We've got men's work to do."

"That deer is mine," the boy said, standing his ground and raising his bow towards the men. "I've been stalking it for over an hour."

"It was my arrow that done the deed, boy," Mall snapped, tiring of the boy's interference. He was just plain tired after the problems of the day. "Stand aside."

"No," the boy snapped. "I'm not letting you take that meat."

Mall chuckled even as Safford rolled his eyes at the orneriness of the boy's reply. "And what'll a little thing like you do about it?"

Safford bent over suddenly, grabbing his shin. "Damn me, but the little bugger just kicked me," he growled.

Mall was letting out a curse of his own, barely ducking the bow that came flying out towards him. "Whoa." He stepped back, watching as the young boy took up a stance with the bow that was threatening. Mall put out his hands, palms up, trying to soothe the youth. "Take it easy, youngin'. Ain't no reason to throw such tantrums. How about we give you a leg to take home to your folks?"

"It's my deer. I'm taking it all," the boy snarled.

"How are you planning on getting it home, boy? There's no way you're going to be able to lift that deer, it weighs more than you do."

"That's none of your concern. You're poaching on the king's lands and killing his deer." He stood straighter, relaxing his guard some. His eyes were riveted upon Mall. "You leave now and I won't report you to King Maxim."

Safford tapped the boy on his shoulder, waiting until he turned, surprised by the sudden appearance of the man. Saff let his fist fly, catching the boy on the chin and watching as he went down instantly.

"Saff, damn man, what are you doing?" Mall dropped his bow, hurrying over to the boy. He put his hand on the boy's face checking his chin. "You could do serious damage, you idiot."

"I pulled the punch, I barely touched him." Saff grinned. He watched as Mall checked his breathing and the bump that grew on his chin. "Bugger it, Mall, quit mother-henning him. He kicked me."

Mall rested his hand on the boy's chest, making sure it rose and fell. His eyes narrowed and he moved his hand on the slender youth. "Fuck me, it can't be," he growled.

"What can't be?" Saff said, Mall's tone telling him something was amiss.

"This boy," he said, "has tits."

* * * *

Look for Mall and Victoria's story and
Gisselle and Saff's from www.melange-books.com